A SINGLE KISS

W WINTERS

Copyright © 2019 by Willow Winters All Rights Reserved.

No part of this publication may be reproduced, stored in a retrieval system, or transmitted in any form or by any means, electronic, mechanical, photocopying, recording, scanning, or otherwise, without the prior written permission of the publisher, except in the case of brief quotations within critical reviews and otherwise as permitted by copyright law.

NOTE: This is a work of fiction.

Names, characters, places, and incidents are a product of the author's imagination.

Any resemblance to real life is purely coincidental. All characters in this story are 18 or older.

Copyright © 2019, Willow Winters Publishing. All rights reserved. willowwinterswrites.com

From *USA Today* best-selling author Willow Winters comes a gripping, heart-wrenching tale of romantic suspense that will keep you on the edge of your seat.

I should feel shame for not wanting this to end, but he doesn't want it to end either.

When the darkness sets in with the flames all flickered out, and the loud click of the locks signal it's over, that's when reality comes flooding back.

The war. The drugs. All of the lies that weave a tangled web for me to get lost in.

I don't want any of it.

I only want him. Jase Cross. My enemy. And yet, the only person I trust.

With broad shoulders and a smoldering look in his dark eyes, Jase is a man born to be powerful.

I shouldn't give him more power than he already has…

Jase Cross will be my downfall.

A Single Kiss is Book 2 of the Irresistible Attraction series. *A Single Glance* must be read first.

"Grief does not change you, Hazel. It reveals you."
—John Green, *The Fault in Our Stars*

A SINGLE KISS

PROLOGUE

Jase

I T'S ODD THE THINGS YOU REMEMBER IN THE midst of fear. Fourteen years later, and I still recall the cracks in the cement; the sidewalks were littered with them. This particular one though… I remember it in vivid detail, probably because of what happened immediately after.

Against the old brick building of the corner store, a green vine had found its way through the broken cement and climbed up the wall. I remember thinking it had no business being there. The crack belonged, but the new life that had sprouted up and borne what looked like a closed flower wasn't supposed to be there. Nothing beautiful belonged on that street.

The dim streetlight revealed how lively it was, even that late at night. With shades of green on the perfect vine and its single leaf with the bud of a flower just waiting to bloom, it made me pause. And in that moment, I hated that it was there.

I was almost eleven and maybe that childishness is why I scraped my shoe against the leaf and stem, ripping and tearing them until the green seemed to bleed against the rough and faded red bricks. I know I wasn't quite eleven, because Mama died right before my birthday that year. It was her medicine that almost fell out of the overfilled paper bag I was gripping so tight as I continued to kick at the wall before feeling all the anger and hate well up and form tears in my eyes.

Life wasn't fair. Back then I was just learning that truth, or at least I'd felt it somewhere deep in my bones, although I hadn't yet said it out loud.

Mama was getting sicker. Dad's condition was getting worse too, although he couldn't use cancer as an excuse. Thinking about the two of them, I continued to kick the wall even though my sneakers were too thin and it hurt to do so. The bottles the clerk had given me to give my dad clinked against one another in the bag, egging me on to keep kicking until I felt a pain that I'd given myself. A pain I deserved.

All the while, the bottles clinked.

That's what I had gone out to get, even as my stomach rumbled. I had enough money left over to get something to eat, but Dad always demanded the receipt. If he saw that I spent his change, I knew it'd be bad. I knew better than to take his money. Times were hard and I would eat what I was given to eat and do what I was told to do.

I picked up the medicine and beer for my folks on the way home from dropping off something at a classmate's house on the other side of town. Maybe a book I'd borrowed.

A SINGLE KISS

Those details are fuzzy over a decade later. I didn't have many friends but a couple of students pitied me. I was the smallest one in the class and we couldn't buy everything I needed for school. The other kids didn't mind letting me borrow their things every once in a while. I never asked the same person in the same week and I always gave stuff back promptly. Mama always smiled when I told her I'd just gotten home from giving things back to my friends. I told her they were my friends, but I knew better. She didn't though.

I'm not sure what I'd returned that night or to who. Only that I had to go by the corner store on the way home.

None of that mattered enough to remember, but the damn flower I'd killed, I remember that.

It was the shame of nearly crying that made me take that detour, right at the damaged sidewalk that was free of what wasn't supposed to be there anymore. I cried a lot and that's why everyone looked at me the way they did. The teachers, the other kids, the clerk at the corner store. They always got a certain look on their faces when they saw the dirty, skinny kid whose mother was dying.

They didn't look at my older brothers that way. They were trouble and I was just... not enough of anything other than a kid to feel sorry for.

I stalked down the alley to hide my face in the darkness, only to meet a man I thought was a figment of everyone's imagination.

He was like the boogeyman or Santa Claus; all myths I didn't believe in.

A lot of people called him the Grim Reaper, but I knew his name was Marcus. It's what my brothers called him. I thought they were messing with me when they'd told me stories about him, right up until I looked into Carter's eyes and he shook my shoulders because I wouldn't listen.

Don't ask for Marcus, don't talk about him. If you hear his name, run the other way. Stay the fuck away from Marcus.

Swallowing thickly, I remember the harsh look of fear that Carter never allowed to cloud his expression and his tone that chilled my spine.

The second I lifted up my head about halfway down that alley, staring at where I'd heard a soft cough in the darkness, in that moment, I knew it was him.

I thought I knew fear before that night. But no monster I'd conjured under the bed ever made my body react like it did when I saw his dark eyes focused on me. His breath fogged in front of him and that was all I could see as my grip involuntarily tightened on the paper bag. It was late, dark and cold. From the icy chill on my skin, down to my blood and even deeper to the core of what makes a person who they are, suddenly it was freezing.

So I stood motionless, paralyzed in place and unable to run even though every instinct inside of me was screaming for me to do so.

I remember how gracefully he jumped down from his perch atop a stack of crates, still hidden in the darkness. The dull thump of his shoes hitting the asphalt made my heart lurch inside of my chest.

"What do you want?" I braved the words without conscious consent. As bitterly cold as I'd been seconds ago, sweat began to bead on my skin. Sweat that burned hotter than I'd ever felt, knowing I dared to speak to a man who would surely kill me before answering my question.

A flash of bright white emerged in the blackness as he

bared a sick grin. I could feel my eyes squint as I searched desperately for his face. I wanted to at least see him, see the man who'd kill me. I'd heard the worst thing you could see before you die was the face of the person who ends your life. But growing up here, I knew it wasn't true. The worst thing you could see were the people all around you who could help, but instead chose to do nothing and continue walking on by.

The streets were quiet behind me, and somewhere deep inside, I was grateful for that. At least if I begged for help, no one would be there to deny me a chance to be saved. It would end and there would be no hope. Having no hope somehow made it better.

"Your brother has an interesting choice of friends."

Again my heart spasmed, pumping hard and violently. *My brother.*

I was going to lose my mother; I knew I would soon. She was holding on as hard as she could, but she'd told me to be strong when the time came and that was a damn hard pill to swallow. I'd already lost what semblance of a father I had.

My brothers…. they were all I had left. I suppose life is meant to be suffered through loss after loss. That would explain why the Grim Reaper showed up, whispering about my brother.

I don't know how I managed to answer him, the man who stayed in the shadows, but I questioned, "Which brother?"

He laughed. It echoed in the narrow alley, a dark and gruff chuckle.

For years that followed, every time I heard footsteps

behind me or thought I saw a figure in the night, I heard that laugh in the depths of my mind. Taunting me.

I heard it again when my mother died, loud and clear as if he was there in that empty kitchen. It was present at her grave, when I saw my closest brother dead in the street, when my father was murdered and I went to identify his body—even when I first killed a man out of vengeance when I was nineteen years old.

That demeaning laugh would haunt me because I knew he was watching. He was watching me die slowly in this wretched world and yet, he did nothing.

"Carter," he finally answered me. "He's making friends he shouldn't."

"How would you know?" I asked without hesitating, even though inside I felt like a twisted rag, devoid of air and feeling.

"I know everything, Jase Cross," he told me, moving closer to me even as I stepped back. The step was quick, too quick and the one free hand I had crashed behind me against the rough brick wall from the liquor shop. It left a small and inconsequential gash just below my middle knuckle. Eventually the gash became a scar, forming a physical memory of Marcus's warning that night. His laugh stayed in my mind after that night, and like my scar, served as a permanent reminder of him over the years.

He neared the dim strip of light from the full moon overhead, the bit that leaked into the alley, but still he didn't show himself.

I nearly dropped the bag in my grasp when he came even closer and I had nowhere to go.

"I have a message for you to deliver to him," he told me.

"If he ever goes against me, your entire family will suffer the consequences."

"Carter?" I breathed his name, shaking my head out of instinct from knowing Carter hadn't done anything. "He doesn't know anyone. You have the wrong person."

All he did was laugh again, the same sick sound coming up from the pit of his stomach. I repeated in the breath of a whisper, "Carter hasn't done anything."

"Not yet, but he will." The words were spoken with such confidence from the darkness. "And I'll be watching."

He left me standing there, on the verge of trembling as he walked away. The pounding in my chest was louder than his quiet footsteps although I didn't dare breathe.

That was the first night I met the man I would now call my enemy. Whatever fear I had for him as a child has turned to resentment and spite.

That's all he is. He's only a man. A man with no face, a hefty bag of threats and a penchant for eliciting fear in all who dare to walk the streets he claims as his own.

These aren't his streets. He has no right to them, but I do.

He treats this world like a game; the lives and deaths of those around us are only pieces on a board to be lost or taken, used however he'd like.

But the mistake he made is simple: He dared to meddle and bring Bethany into this game.

She's mine. Only mine.

Not a pawn for him to play with.

It's time for Marcus's game to end.

CHAPTER 1

Bethany

Fuck. Fuck. Fuck. Fuck. Fuck.
A numb prickle of fear races up and down my body like a thousand needles keeping me still. All the while, my heart's the only thing that's moving. It's frantic and unyielding as it thrashes inside of me.

The floorboards creak again as someone moves toward the stairs while I keep my feet firmly planted in the kitchen. *Someone.* Who? I don't know.

No one has ever walked into my home unannounced and I know it's not Laura; I know it's not Jase. Just thinking his name sends another chill down my spine. The fear, the regret, the unknown from what I just read in The Coverless Book are all things I can't dwell on right now. Blinking furiously, I shut the wayward trail of thoughts down.

No, it's not Jase.

It's someone else, someone with bad intentions. Deep down, I can feel it.

If I'd just been back in the living room when the door opened, back there where I was a moment ago, reading The Coverless Book and using this notebook to jot down the underlined words... if I'd been there, whoever just opened the door would have seen me instantly. If I'd left the notebook in the living room, and not in the drawer in the kitchen, whoever it was, would have seen me. I wouldn't have had a chance to run.

Fate spared me, but for how long?

My fingers tremble as I silently set the notebook down on the counter, devising a plan.

Get my phone. Run the hell out of here. Call the cops.

It's as simple as that. If I can't get the phone, *just run.*

Whoever it is, they're heading upstairs and once I hear the creaking from the floorboards move from the stairs to one of the bedrooms, I'll move as quickly and quietly as possible. I can barely keep it together while I'm waiting, listening, and feeling the numbing fear flowing over my skin.

Hot and cold sensations overwhelm my body at once and I don't know how I'm even capable of breathing with how tight and raw and dry my throat is. All I know is that I can't fail. I can't let him know where I am.

My movements are measured as I release the notebook. The second I do, I hear another person open my front door. *Thump, thump, thump.* My heartbeat is louder than anything else. Another person's here. I'm not in control as I instinctively back away from the threshold of the kitchen, closer toward the back of the house.

One person and then another.

A SINGLE KISS

Thump, thump, thump.

Abandoning all reason, I turn my back to where they are, ready to hide somewhere as quickly as possible. *Somewhere. Where? Where can I hide?* My head whirls with panic. I need to hide.

My body freezes when I hear my phone go off. It's still where I left it in the next room over, the living room. Footsteps come closer, closer to me, closer to the threshold of the kitchen where they can see me. *No, fuck, please no.* Inwardly I beg; I plead.

I'm trapped in the narrow kitchen with three people sneaking into my home. I can't die here. Not like this. Not after everything that's happened. It would be more than cruel to make me suffer in the last weeks of my life, like this.

I know if whoever it is stops at the coffee table where my phone is, he won't be able to see into the galley kitchen, but that won't stop him from moving on once he picks up my cell. Even more, he'll know for certain I'm here. I wouldn't leave without my phone, so they'll know. *Fuck!*

Thump, thump, thump. I wish I could quiet the pulse that's banging in my ears faster by the second.

Forcing myself to calm down and think as I hear a murmur from only ten... maybe twelve feet away in the other room, I focus on anywhere I could conceal myself. The pantry is the obvious solution, but it's so full, there's no way. Plus the shelves come out too far.

With numb fingers, I pry open the cabinet door for the recycling. The bin is still outside where I left it for pickup yesterday. It'll be cramped, but I think I can squeeze myself into the small space. I don't know the chances they'd open every cabinet of the kitchen, but I don't have anywhere else to hide.

My feet are heavy and my limbs rigid. I'm not as quiet as I wish I was. But I'm quick. I'm damn quick as I cram myself inside of the cabinet, the faint scent of spilled wine that's leaked from empty bottles hitting me at full force, along with other less than desirable odors.

I couldn't give two shits about what it smells like. All I care about is if they heard. *Please, please.* The telltale sound of shoes on the tile lets me know someone's here.

The weight of the steps is heavy; they have to be from a man. Both hands cover my mouth out of an instinct to be quiet, just as my eyes slam shut tight and refuse to look. I pray he didn't hear. If he heard the sound of a cabinet… *fuck. Please, no.*

I swear whoever it is can hear my ragged breaths and the ringing in my ears that's so fucking loud I can barely hear them walk into the kitchen. Them. Multiple footsteps.

Fuck, fuck, fuck, fuck.

I can't think about it. I can't be here right now. Not my mind. The stress and fear wrap around my body like barbed wire, tightening by the second and forcing me to fight it, to move, to react. I can't be here. This can't be happening.

Go somewhere else. My own words, words I've told patients many times slip into my consciousness. *Go somewhere else.*

"Have you ever thought about what it would be like to be pregnant?" my mother asks me with a devious grin. Her knee rocks back and forth as she sits in the chair, playing with her long hair that's draped over one shoulder. "Like, to

be Talia right now? Could you imagine?"

I was hoping she'd remember today, but at least she's talking. That's good, I tell myself. It's good that she's happy today, in whatever time she's living in, it was a happy one for her.

"Who's Talia?" I ask her, feigning the curiosity I think she'd expect from whoever it is she thinks she's talking to. It's never me. She never knows it's me.

"You know, the blonde in Mr. Spears's class. She's almost six months along now," my mother says, enjoying the gossip.

"Mr. Spears?"

"Tenth grade English. The really tall one and kind of young? I think he's hot."

My mother's comment makes me smile. I wish I were back in high school. She didn't have Alzheimer's then.

"So have you thought about it?" she questions again and I shake my head honestly.

"I can't imagine having kids right now."

"I can. I want a boy. A boy with James Peters's eyes and smile."

"James Peters." I repeat the boy's name and set two cups of water down on the end table.

"One day I'm going to ask him out."

"What if you have a girl?" I ask her.

"Oh no," she says and shakes her head. "Girls are too much trouble." I have to remind myself that she's only a teenager today. I'm sure all teenagers think that. They have perceptions before having kids.

I remind myself of it but still, I have to get up and get away. Just for a minute.

"Where are you going? Is class starting soon? I thought

we had another half hour of lunch?"

"We do," I answer her, forcing a smile. "I just have to do something."

"You forgot your books, didn't you, Maggie?" She taunts me. "You're so forgetful."

I can feel it when I hit my breaking point. It's not getting easier like I thought it would.

Resting against the wall in the kitchen, all I can do is breathe. All I can do is hide from my mother and hide from the truth.

"Does Mom remember?" Jenny's question comes from the threshold of the kitchen. She leans against it with a mug in her hand although I can smell the whiskey from here. I'm not sure if it's in her mug or just a leftover stench from wherever she was last night.

"No," I answer her.

She takes a sip in response and with it, I'm given an answer to my own unspoken question. It's nine in the morning and the whiskey is in the cup she's currently clinging to.

"She's talking about having kids right now. Back in high school."

"Kids," my sister repeats, rolling her eyes and taking another sip.

"Yeah, she said she wants daughters." I don't know why the lie slipped out. I think I just wanted to comfort my sister.

My sister throws the mug back, downing its contents before tossing it into the sink.

"Really? She told me the other day she'd hate to have daughters."

A bang close by brings me back to now. Back to the present. Away from my sister and away from my mother.

My eyes open unhurriedly, not wanting to see but forcing myself to take in anything I can in the dark space. Tremors run through my legs and up my spine to my shoulders, leaving goosebumps in their wake. With a single unsteady exhale, I stare through the bright slit in the cabinet door as faded, broken-in blue jeans show themselves. I can see the seams and the stitching even. He's that close to me. Just behind the door. I nearly whimper when the creak of the pantry closet proves he's searching for me.

He heard me moving around in the kitchen. I feel lightheaded for a moment, maybe from fear, maybe from holding my breath.

A buzzing from the other room makes him turn on his heels and I watch all the while with both hands over my mouth, my palms sweaty and clammy. He stands still as the other person walks out of the kitchen. They're louder now, reckless and bold as they open doors and search for something or someone.

It doesn't have to be me. Please, don't let what they're looking for be me. Be looking for something Jenny left here. Please, for the love of God, be that. Find it. Find it and get out.

The thoughts don't go unanswered. Fate lets me know the worst-case scenario is in fact my reality.

"Her car is still in the driveway. You think she heard us and ran?" A muted voice I don't recognize is coming from the living room. Another voice, one from farther away, maybe in the foyer answers, "Nah, she has to be here still. She wouldn't leave her phone."

The man just beyond the cabinet door walks away swiftly and moves toward the voice—that's when I catch a glimpse of the red stripes on his white sneakers. A single horizontal stripe runs along the length of each shoe midway up the side. White shoes with red stripes. I can hear him smack the man after a gruff response from his throat and then it's quiet again.

The man who was so close to me knows better than to talk and give away their thoughts.

Thump, thump, thump. They don't say another word as I inhale the musty smells from the cabinetry, willing my body to obey me and not betray my position.

Every time a loud bang or the crash of something being overturned startles me, my shoulders push harder against the rough wood behind my back and I bite down on the inside of my cheek to silence the instinctive scream.

My nails dig deeper into my skin on my thighs as the bangs get closer and louder. It's obvious they're trashing the place. All the while, I pray. *Please don't find me. Please leave.*

For a moment, I think they might.

The recognizable noise of the front door opening is suddenly clear. As are the sounds of them leaving, one by one, but I don't believe they're truly gone. It's too obvious. It's a trick and a trap; one I won't be caught in. Time passes, each second seeming longer and longer, gauged by the steady ticking of the clock above the kitchen sink.

All I can think about is every time a girl is in the middle of the woods running from someone in the movies. She hides behind a tree or bush—something that offers her a hidden spot—and she waits until she thinks they've run by and can't hear them anymore. She thinks they've moved on, as if they've kept running through the tall trees and didn't see her. She doesn't hear them, so she takes off.

That's when they catch her. They know she's hiding and they're just waiting until she comes out to snatch her up.

Not me. They won't catch me that way. For the first time since I heard someone come in, strength and conviction outweigh the fear. I'll stay here until I know for certain it's safe.

I don't know what these men wanted with me, but I know they were looking for me and that's all the reason I need to stay right where I fucking am.

My body stays tense for I don't even know how long. It feels like maybe ten minutes. Only ten minutes or so, maybe twenty? I can't track the sound of the clock; it's going too fast and then too slow and then it blurs together and I can't focus on it. It feels hotter and hotter in this small space, but I don't waver. Never daring to move. Not even after it's silent. With stiff legs and an aching back, I finally lower my hands and that's when I realize how my neck is bent. It hurts; everything hurts from being shoved in this small space and hunched over, crouched down. My ankle dares to stretch forward, causing my toes to brush against the cabinet door.

Did they really leave?

Not a sound is heard when the cabinet pushes open, ever so slightly. I didn't do it on purpose, I just needed to move.

Nothing happens. There's no sign they're still here and I could see myself sneaking out slowly, risking a look.

I still don't trust it though. What happens if they're right outside and they see through the windows that I'm here? A black vision passes before my eyes and my head falls back, feeling the anxiety rush through me.

Staying as still and as silent as I can be, I wait, praying for a sign that I'm safe.

All I'm given is silence. God didn't answer my prayers for my sister. Why would he answer me now?

For the longest time, there's nothing but silence. The tick of the clock goes on and on, and I endure it. Not daring to move.

And then everything happens all at once.

The slam of the front door, and then the back door to the garage. My hands whip up to my mouth to cover the silent scream as my entire body tenses and my skin scrapes against the wooden walls of my hiding spot.

The crash of glass breaking, I think a window in the back room, makes my shoulders hunch and I wish I could hide even further back. All of it is followed by the sound of tires squealing from outside my house. At least two cars. At least three men. And one with a pair of white shoes with red stripes.

I don't think I inhale the entire time. It doesn't seem like they came back in. They merely broke something from the outside. Did they throw something inside the house? A bomb? That's the first place my head goes. They threw a bomb in here and I'm going to die anyway. Still, I can't move and nothing happens.

There's no noise, no explosion. Just silence again.

Possibilities run furiously through my mind as I try to calm down. The back of my head rests against the wood as my thoughts turn dark. I think about how desperate I was to move, and how they were right there waiting. How close I was to playing into their trap.

I don't have long to drown in gratitude and the horror of what could have been. Maybe five or ten minutes go by before I hear another car. That's all the time that passes from the squeal of one set of tires leaving and then the shriek of another set slamming to a halt in front of my house.

I nearly upheave at the prospect of what they came back to do.

The front door opens, loud with intention, banging off the wall. Then I faintly hear a gun cock, followed by his voice.

Jase.

"Bethany!" Although he screams my name with a demand, his cadence is laced with panic. "Bethany, where are you?" he calls out as I hear the crunch of glass beneath his feet. "Fuck! Bethany!" He screams my name louder and still I don't move.

There's a moment where I feel relief. Where I want to run to him and get out of here, climbing into his arms and begging him to take me away from here and spilling everything.

But then I remember. The black words on cream paper with the blue underlined ink left from Jenny. All I can think about is how CROSS was in The Coverless Book. A hidden message from my sister.

The unknowing fear is crippling and the pain in my chest makes me grip my shirt, right where it's hurting.

I hear the faint sound of a phone dialing—muted and barely heard, followed by my cell vibrating on the coffee table. *They left it?*

"Fuck!" Jase screams and then hurls something across

my living room that makes my entire body jostle.

My thoughts scramble, my emotions stay at war with one another, but one thing is for certain: He'll protect me. The selfish thought forces me to lurch from where I am.

I push the cabinet door open, the creaking a companion to the aching pain of my muscles screaming from being cramped up for so long. "Jase." I try to call out his name, but it comes out jagged and hoarse from my dry throat. I fall on my ass and right thigh as I make my way out of the cabinet, wincing from a cramp sending a sharp pain shooting up my side just as Jase sees me.

"Bethany," he says, and my name is wretched on his lips. Slipping out with relief and his own fears ringing through.

I'm stiff as he drops to his knees beside me, pulling me into his hard chest. Both of his arms wrap around me and he tucks my head under his chin, rocking me and kissing my hair. I can't focus on him though; my body is screaming in pain. I just want to breathe and stand up. Why do I hurt so much? I don't know what to think or what to say or what to do. It's all too much. I'm breaking down.

All I can focus on is keeping my eyes open and staying aware. He's still shushing me when I finally push a logical thought out.

"Let me go," I tell him, my words rushed. I have to clear my throat, but that just makes it more hoarse. My body's still stiff and it's then that Jase seems to notice I'm not quivering in his arms and begging for him to save me. Maybe that's what I should have done, but I've always been a bad liar. "I need to move; let me go."

The change in Jase's demeanor is immediate and palpable. His grip moves to my upper arms, his fingers digging into my flesh and nearly hurting me.

"What happened? Are you okay?" he questions and the hardness in his words echoes the look in his gaze. Piercing me, demanding information. He doesn't let go. There's no sympathy from him, and for the first time, I see the man he really is. The man who rules with fear and unrelenting force.

I try to answer him, but my throat is so dry I could choke on the words. With a heavy breath out, I feel faint, staring into his eyes. I watch as his stern expression changes slowly. Before, I felt like I'd been given a glimpse, but thought I'd imagined it. This time I know I saw it.

"Why didn't you answer me?" The words of his question waver. The guilt and betrayal flicker on each syllable and make my chest feel hollow and vacant. I'm pinned by his gaze and the nausea comes back full force.

A dry heave breaks the tension, forcing Jase to lift me to my feet and bring me to the sink. Pushing him away with one shaking hand, I turn the faucet on, my fingers slipping around the knob at first, unable to grip it tight enough. The cold water is more than a relief against my face, dripping down my neck and throat, even though it soaks into my sweater. And then drinking it from my cupped hands. I hear Jase go through a cabinet to my upper left and then he pushes a glass toward me for me to take.

One breath. And another. One breath. And another. The water swirls around the drain and I focus on two things.

1. I'm alive.
2. Jase doesn't know about the message in the book.

It's hard to remember where we were before I read those lines. It's always hard going back.

The knob protests with a squeaking sound as I turn it off, still not daring to look Jase in the eyes. Leaning my hip against the countertop to stay upright, I force myself to calm down. Still feeling dizzy and as if I don't have a grasp on anything at all, bringing my arms up to cross in front of me, I spit it out, one line at a time.

"At first one man... or woman," I breathe the words out. "I didn't know who it was but..." I trail off slowly, because that's when I remember Jase said he wasn't coming over tonight. I knew it wasn't him because he'd told me he wasn't coming.

"Why are you here?" I ask him and stare into his dark eyes as I feel how heavy my own are.

"Things changed and I wanted to make sure you were all right." Every word is spoken with a sense of calm but also forcefully. His hand on my upper arm steals my attention. Though gentle, it's demanding just the same. It strikes me that "gentle but demanding" is exactly how I'd describe this man. The knowledge makes something in the pit of my stomach flicker to life, a dull burn.

"One man came? One man did all of this?" he questions.

One breath, one beat of my heart and I move my gaze to his. "I was in the kitchen and heard someone come in. Whoever it was went upstairs and before I could do anything, two more people came in and I hid."

It sounds so simple when I say it like that. Only two sentences to describe the last half hour? Or maybe an hour? I peek at the oven and then swallow thickly at the red digital numbers staring back at me. Over an hour and a half. Sucking in a hesitant breath and closing my eyes, I tell him just that. "I hid for an hour and a half and they just left."

My eyes are still closed when he asks, "They just left? How long ago?"

The irritation that flows from my words is unjustified, but it's there nonetheless. "Yes, that's what I just said. They just left." My voice cracks as I raise it and pull the hair away from my hot face. "Minutes ago. They could come back." I lie and say, "That's why I couldn't answer you when you first came in. I wasn't sure if they were really gone yet."

He sees right through my lie; I can tell with the hint of a tilt of his head.

The realization leaves me just as it comes. Jase is here. Relief is hesitant to console me when he says, "No one's going to hurt you," instead of calling me out on the lie.

"You sound so sure of that," I speak just under my breath and finally look into his eyes. Into the eyes of a man I was falling for. A man I trusted and slept with. A man who makes me question everything now.

I have to break his gaze and let out an uneasy breath as I stare past him and see the destruction. "Oh my God." The words fall from my lips. "What the hell did they do?"

He follows me silently as I walk without thinking into the living room. The sofa is moved away from the wall, the cushions scattered on the floor. Maybe they did that when they were searching for me, but the lamp is busted, the light bulb shattered on the floor where it fell, the coffee table is overturned and that's when I realize the book is gone.

The Coverless Book. Disbelief runs through me in a

wave as I fall to the floor searching for it, but knowing it's not here.

These were my mother's things and the first pieces of furniture I bought on my own. Pieces I picked out with my sister. Each and every thing in this house comes with a memory. They violated it. I've never felt like this before.

"A robbery," Jase says behind me and I shake my head. Denying the lie he speaks.

"They wanted it to look like that." I'm barely conscious of my response as I take in the place. "That's why they did it," I add as the thought hits me and I stand up, looking toward the door. "They broke the window after they left to make it look like a robbery. Like they broke the glass to unlock the door."

I feel sickened more than angered.

Pushing the hair out of my face, I try to think about what they could have been after, but it's obvious. "They came here for me, but they thought I ran, so they made it look like a break-in." I whip around to face Jase and tell him, "They knew I was here... or maybe they thought I took off. So they staged it..." My gaze falls as I swallow the lump in my throat. "They thought I took off when I heard them so they staged it as a robbery."

"It's a setup," Jase agrees, searching through things and telling me Seth is nearby watching the entrance to the neighborhood and that everything's okay now. He promises me he'll fix it, he says he'll find whoever it was and make them pay. He tells me he's happy I'm okay and tries to comfort me with his touch, but I pull away. I don't listen to his promises. I'm not in the habit of relying on promises. The seconds pass as I give myself a moment to actually process what happened.

It makes sense. All of it makes sense.

But why take the book? Every hair on the back of my neck stands up when the question echoes in my head.

My phone's on the floor, as is a stack of envelopes from the pile of opened mail, but the mail itself, is missing. They were only bills, nothing of importance. But my laptop is gone too. Fuck! I need that for work. As I halfheartedly lean forward searching through my things, I take everything into account, but the one thing that matters... It really isn't here.

"The book." I can't help but to say it out loud and when I do, my lips feel chapped and the sentence comes out raw. "They took it?" Denial is apparent. "Why take the book?" I shove everything out of the way, searching all over the living room until I get to the hallway only to see it's trashed too. My mother's vase sits perfectly where it is, thank God, but the light in the hall is broken. All the lights are broken.

They upturned the furniture, then busted the lights and stole meaningless items with no worth. Meaningless to them, but to me... "I want my book back." I'm surprised that after all this time, the back of my eyes prick and my hands ball into fists at the thought of someone coming in here and taking The Coverless Book.

I don't even realize I'm shaking until Jase holds me from behind, pulling me into his chest. And again, I'm stiff.

His embrace is calming and masculine, wrapped in warmth. It's designed to comfort, just like the small kiss he plants on my neck. But I can't relax. I can't.

"Why did they do this?" My question turns to broken pieces of whispered syllables in the air.

"Stay with me. I'll make sure we find them and get your book back." His soothing words do nothing to change what's happened and where my mind leads me.

None of this would have happened if Jenny hadn't died; if she hadn't gotten herself into this mess. It always leads back to Jenny and with her name on the tip of my tongue, tears threaten again to fall.

All the calm words and pretty promises couldn't keep the tremors at bay.

"I want to know who they were. They knew what they were doing. It's the men who murdered Jenny. That's why they took the book."

Every memory of my sister always brings out the worst in me.

Angry tears form but don't fall as I take in a heavy breath and shove Jase away. I'm good at doing that. At shoving people away.

Those bastards came here. They took her book from me, the last thing she left me and the only thing that had a message from her. The only key I had to finding out what happened to her.

"Call the cops," I demand, wiping at my eyes with the sleeve of my sweater. The words scratch my throat on their way out.

"No." He answers hard.

"Call them!" I screech, shoving my fists into Jase's chest to get him away from me. Anger is nothing compared to what I feel. He grabs my wrists quicker than I can register, forcing me to stare up at him. He can stare all he wants; he can try to hold me, try to bend me to his will, nothing will get through to me. Once he learns that, he'll leave.

A SINGLE KISS

It's only when I look into his eyes in this foyer, with this fear and the memories of Jenny that I realize it's just as it was a week and a half ago when he first knocked on my door. Nothing has changed.

"Just go," I seethe.

"Calm down." He grits the words through his teeth, the irritation barely contained in his voice.

"I'm calling the cops." I stare into his eyes as I speak.

"No, you're not. You're going to come with me. You're going to wait while I find the men who did this and make this right." Every word from his mouth is a demand. They strike me and dare me not to obey.

Ripping my hands away from him, I step back and then step back again. My teeth grind so hard against one another they could crack.

Jase knows better than to approach me as I reach for my shoes and then gather my phone without a word spoken. He thinks I'm obeying him. Going along with what he says and listening like a good girl.

Never in my life has someone bossed me around and told me what to do. Not until Jenny went away and Jase came storming into my life. The bitter acknowledgement stays with me as I prepare to get the hell away from here.

He walks around my place as I silently put on my shoes and grab my coat, my car keys still in the right pocket. Beneath the heavy fabric is my purse, the wallet still there.

And the knowledge is a smack in the face.

They had to know it would be obvious that it wasn't a robbery. Maybe they were counting on me not calling the police. Maybe they know about Jase. They thought I'd run to him?

A chill flows down my spine as I stare up at the man I've been sleeping with, the man I thought I was falling for. He nods toward the door, telling me he has to make a call before we leave.

I don't answer him, not trusting myself to speak.

Instead, while he's on the phone on the porch I walk right past his car and get into my own, speeding off quickly enough so that all he can do is run into the street as I stare into my rearview mirror watching him.

The deafening silence is my only companion as I run away from it all, toward God knows where. I have no idea where I'm going or how I'll find a way out of this mess. The second I get around the corner, panic takes over. Realizing this is my life; this is what my life has become.

The tires screech as I yank the wheel to the left and turn into the neighbor's long drive. Slamming on the brakes and parking, I turn off the car, feeling a sickness churn in my gut.

I did what she used to do to me.

This is what Jenny used to do when she'd leave in an angry fit. We'd get into fights about her new friends and new habits. She'd threaten to leave and I'd threaten to follow. She thought I didn't know that she would just pull in here until things calmed down and then she'd drive home. She'd drive away, just to hide down the street, all alone crying in her car. The house itself is empty. The owner lives in a retirement home and his kids aren't willing to sell it yet.

I knew. I knew exactly what Jenny was doing. Not the first time, but the time after, she was too slow and I saw. I'd drive past every time though and park a few streets down and then walk back up here, watching her cry in the driver's seat. At least she was safe.

That's all I ever wanted.

Safe is what matters.

That's what I told myself back then. As I see Jase speed down the road behind me, not glancing my way at all, that's what I tell myself now. I need to keep myself safe. Safe from everything.

I don't trust anyone.

All I know is that I need my book back.

I need to know what Jenny's last words to me were.

CHAPTER 2

Jase

THE LEATHER IS HOT AGAINST MY PALMS AS I twist my hands around the steering wheel. My knuckles are turning white with every second that passes.

I force myself to focus on every detail around me to keep from losing all sense of control.

The ringing of Seth's phone echoes in the silent car. It rings once, then halfway through a second ring before he picks up.

"Where is she?" My question comes out hard and I don't bother to hide the fury. "How the fuck did she get away?"

"Boss?" Seth questions and it only makes the irritation grow.

A seething anger is in command of every aspect of

my being right now. Nothing is going right and nothing is under control. "Where the fuck is she?" I scream the question, feeling each word claw up my throat on the way out.

"Bethany Fawn's car is located at Forty-two Bayview."

"Forty-two Bayview." I breathe out the address, craning my neck beneath the windshield to look at the small green street sign and then to my left as if one of them will magically be Bayview. Neither of them are and that fact is why I slam my fist on the dashboard as I simmer with pure rage. She fucking left me. Knowing there are men after her, she fucking ran from me!

"Four streets behind you, Mr. Cross." I focus on what I can control and then finally breathe.

"Four streets?" I swallow after repeating what he said, knowing she's safe. She's within reach.

"Make a U-turn when you're able. It looks like she stayed there for..." The word stretches out as he pauses and then continues, "...two minutes. She's on the move now, backing out of the driveway." Seth uses the GPS in her car to track her and gives me directions. "I'm still at the back entrance to the neighborhood and it looks like she's coming this way. She'll be driving by me if she stays on course."

"Follow her." Resolution takes over, following a pang of regret. Running my hand down my face and pinching the bridge of my nose, I try to pinpoint the moment I lost her. Truly lost her. She shouldn't have done that. Something happened.

The break-in. I slam my head back, exhaling a tight breath and loathing the life I live. No shit, something happened. What the fuck is wrong with me?

"On her tail," Seth says over the speaker. His obliviousness to my state is a kind gift in this moment as I press my palms to my eyes and focus on what I can do to keep her safe.

"Call for backup and continue following her but keep your distance and keep me informed. I want to know where she's going and I never want her out of your sight."

"Understood, Boss."

"I'm not letting her go," I tell him. My voice is firm and resolute, although my words are more for me than for him.

"Of course not," he answers although his tone has changed. Softer, not consoling, but understanding. A sedan skirts around me, a newer Mazda with an older man at the wheel who looks at me with a crease marred into his wrinkled forehead as his car passes mine.

Forcing a semblance of a smile to my lips, I offer him a small wave and pretend to be someone just passing by. As if I could ever just pass by Bethany. I would never be able to not feel her presence in a crowded room. I could never ignore it. Let alone allow her to ignore me.

"Is everything all right?" Seth asks after a moment of quiet.

"No, I'll brief you once she's secure."

There's a pause before he asks, "Is there anything else I can do?"

"She is your only priority at the moment."

It's quiet again, but I can't hang up yet. Not without Seth acknowledging what I just said. My gaze lifts to the rearview as a man exits his front door. As he walks to the car in his driveway, the headlights flash and it's only then that I'm aware of how dark it's gotten.

It wasn't that late when I left the cemetery. I just wanted to make sure she was okay. It was foolish to think she would be.

It took me far too long to get to her. I never would have guessed when I got there that her brunette hair would tumble into a halo upon the tiled floor, followed by her small frame. My hand stings from the impact of bashing it against the dashboard a moment ago and I clench it into a tight fist, staring at the silver scar below my knuckle as I remember how she fell.

Fuck, she didn't even make a sound for the longest second.

I thought she was dead. I thought he'd killed her. I thought Marcus had ripped her away from me, getting to her first, when she fell out onto the kitchen floor. I hate that the scar stares back at me in this moment.

It's hard to ignore the splinter of pain that tears through me.

Why else would she not have responded? He'd killed her and shoved her in a cabinet for me to find. I thought it was merely her body falling and that she was already dead.

"Does she know about Jenny?" Seth's question brings me back to the present. To her running away from me.

"That he has her?" I clarify and breathe in deep, staring at the picket fence in front of me. "She doesn't know anything. I didn't tell her about the note."

She'll live her life with unanswered questions unless I can give them to her, and right now, I wouldn't be so cruel.

Even if she'd been fine. Even if she'd spilled out of that

cabinet and ran to me like I wanted her to, I wouldn't tell her. She's barely holding on as it is. It's not pity I feel for her, it's worry.

"I'm not telling her that her sister's alive until I know we can bring her back." It's one mess after the other. "False hope can kill what's left of a person." That's the only explanation I give him. He knows about the note from Marcus. He knows Marcus has Jenny.

I'd rather she continue thinking Jenny's dead. Just in case that's how this all ends.

"We'll discuss everything moving forward tonight." Even as I give him the command, I hear the fatigue in my voice. The day has taken its toll. More than its fair share. "Has my brother gotten in touch with you?"

"About the men we sent out?" he asks to clarify.

"Yes."

"We have men trailing the man seen with Jenny. His name's Luke Stevens. He's driving out west. We don't know where to but he's definitely taken orders from Marcus. He's mentioned him twice on the calls taken from his car."

"Don't let him get far; I don't give a shit if we blow our cover. Have our men grab him and bring him back here."

"Consider it done."

"Good. I want him brought in and questioned. I want to know everything about Marcus. About Jenny. Everything that bastard knows... I'll get it from him." There are enemies everywhere and everything is moving quickly. "Bethany needs to stay put tonight. Let her run it off. But stay on her and don't lose her. I want an update every five minutes."

"Of course," he answers me.

A SINGLE KISS

Glancing at the clock, I change my mind. "Every three minutes. An update every three minutes." I give him the order as I make a U-turn and head back to Bethany's home, preparing myself for the evidence of what happened. "Briefing is tonight, war starts tomorrow."

CHAPTER 3

Bethany

I SHOULDN'T CALL LAURA. I KEEP THINKING IT over and over again even as I stare at the bright white screen of my phone with her contact info staring back at me.

I'm so fucking alone. After driving to nowhere in silence for an hour, that's what I've realized more than anything. I'm so fucking alone.

It's sad when you realize there's only one person left, and you can't reach out to them, because God forbid if what happened to me affects her. I'd never forgive myself.

The darkness outside drifts in as I sit listless in the driver's seat. There's not a star in the black sky and the moon is merely a sliver. Not even the lingering snow reflects the light. It's no longer white and bright, it's dulled and nearly vanished as well.

My teeth scrape against my bottom lip as I pull it into my mouth and look out of my window, still strapped in to the driver's seat. From the outside of my house, no one would ever know what happened.

Closed doors hide a variety of crimes.

Wiping under my tired, burning eyes, I then press the button to exit my contacts to prevent myself from giving in and being weak. I won't call her.

But that only leaves Jase.

CROSS. I can't think of him without being reminded of the book, the underlined hidden message inside it, followed by the break-in, and then Jenny. Every thought, question, and mournful memory assault me one after the other just from thinking his name. I'm so confused and lost... and alone.

I stare down at the white plastic bag on the passenger seat. The logo of Martin Hardware stares back at me in a bold red font and beneath it I know there are three packs of light bulbs, each containing four apiece. It took me a while to feel safe enough to go in. Shit, it took me a while to stop looking in my rearview mirror and keeping track of cars who could be following me. There was no one there for all the hours I've been away from my home.

There's no one here now either. It's just me and the aftermath.

All I have to do is get out of my car and replace the bulbs so I can at least turn on a light.

I have to know what happened. I have to search my place and see what they took. The puzzle keeps me from breaking down. It keeps me from remembering Jenny and the fact that she's gone. As well as Jase, and the fact that he may be to blame if the message in the book is about him.

Why did they take the book and my bills? I think back to the living room. Everything turned over, but systematically. Everything was done with the purpose of making it look like a robbery... but they didn't steal what a random burglar would take.

A long exhale and I'm able to pretend like it isn't devastating. Like I don't feel violated. Like there's no reason for me to be terrified.

My bills and mail, plus whatever other papers were in the coffee table, although I can't even imagine what else I had stored there. And my laptop.

But not my phone or my wallet.

They stole information.

Resting my elbow against the window frame of my car, I press my thumbnail between my teeth and bite down gently, mindlessly. All I can do is stare at my front door and see a man. He had to have been tall, wearing faded, broken-in blue jeans and white sneakers with a red stripe along the sides of each. My mind plays the scene for me. Him quietly picking the lock, pressing his shoulder against the door and opening it as silently as he could. Did he know I was in the living room before he stepped in? Did he peek into the curtains in the bay window beforehand?

Again the series of thoughts plays out. The break-in will always lead to Jenny.

Did he hurt Jenny? Did he know her? I can barely stand to look at the stark white door as the realization hits me.

The men I've been after, the ones I've demanded

be served justice were only feet from me today. And I cowered.

My breathing comes in staggered pants as I look at my front door again and instead of seeing him, I see my sister sitting on the front step. Just as she was the last time I saw her. Bloodshot eyes full of fear staring back at me. It was the day she gave me the gun.

The image washes away as my eyes turn glossy, but the emotions are short lived.

Bright lights from a passing car distract me and the fear I can't deny takes over. It lasts only for a second as the car continues on its way, never even turning down this street.

The sliver of strength I had pulling into the driveway is long gone.

The adrenaline doesn't wane though. And I know there's no way I can go back inside.

I can't sleep here.

I'll never feel safe in this house again.

My thoughts aren't cohesive when I call him. I don't even realize what I've done until Jase's phone is ringing with my cell pressed to my ear. He doesn't make me wait long to answer. Which is a damn good thing, because I nearly hang up on the second ring.

"Bethany." He says my name with a quiet emotion I can't quite place. Longing is evident though and somehow that makes me feel like it's all going to be okay. But how could it ever be okay at this point?

Time goes by and words evade me. Jase doesn't speak either.

"Are you angry?" I eventually ask him and I can't

fathom why. It shouldn't matter if he's angry at me or not. My life does not revolve around this dark knight. I won't allow it. I don't want this life.

"I'm disappointed."

"You sound like my mother," I answer with feigned sarcasm and not really meaning it. It just seems like something someone would say in response to, *I'm disappointed*.

All I can hear is a huff on the end of the line followed by a resigned sigh. "I keep having to remind myself that you're going through a lot, but that doesn't mean you can do this shit, Bethany."

Shame heats my cheeks and my throat dries, keeping me from being able to swallow as I look back to the house. With every passing second, I'm sinking deeper into the dark pit of emotions that's expanding around me.

"You don't know what I'm going through," I tell him simply. And all the voices I've heard before at the hospital echo in my mind. So many people think no one else feels the way they do when they're mourning, when they're sick. When life has got them by the throat and they have nowhere else to turn to but a mental hospital.

"I know people have it worse, people have more pain and more tragedy... but that doesn't mean I'm not handling things the best way that I can." Dignity is slow to greet me and I strengthen my voice to tell him, "I'm trying to just hold on right now." As I finish, my words crack and it's then that I feel as crazy as my patients. I'm losing it. I'm losing everything, watching it all slip through my fingers like the sand of an hourglass.

"Why did you run?" he asks me, not commenting on a word I've just spoken. Somehow, I'm grateful for that.

"I wasn't in the right mindset to be bossed around and whisked away." It's semi-honest. At the very least, it's not a lie.

"And now?"

"I don't know what to do," I admit, feeling the insecurity and the weight of what's happened push against my chest. "And I'm scared," I add. The confession barely leaves me; I don't know if he heard me or not. Another car passes down the street that crosses mine, forming a T-shaped intersection. This time I'm not as scared, but I'm conscious of it. I'm conscious of everything around me.

"Do you want to stay with me?" he asks.

"No," I say, and it hurts to answer him honestly. Physically hurts and drains me of what little strength I have left. I should add that I don't trust him after what I read in the book. But without the book, I can't be certain that I shouldn't trust him. Which makes everything all the more complicated.

"Why is that?" There's no hint of what he's feeling in his question; it's only a string of words asked for clarity. And that makes it easier, but not easy enough to tell the truth. How could I tell him I saw his last name in a coded message in The Coverless Book? I already feel like I've gone insane. I don't need someone else to confirm it.

"I'm just confused and I want to be alone." Nodding to myself although he can't see me, I repeat the sentiment, "I'm not sure exactly what I want right now, but I think I'd really like to be alone."

"I'd prefer you weren't alone right now… And you still owe me time." He adds the second statement when I don't respond to the first.

"I can always say no."

"I never should have put that in the contract."

His response forces a weak smile to my face. It's just as tired and sad as I am. "Your contract is bullshit." Our quips are a quick tit for tat. The rough chuckle from the other end of the line eases a small piece of me. As if slowly melting a large sheet of ice that encases and presses against me constantly.

"You're not going to be happy." He pauses after his statement and I simply wait for what's next, not responding until I know what he's getting at.

"Seth is behind you. He's parked a few houses down. I'll have him flash his lights for you." *Thump*, my heart squeezes tight, so tight it hurts and I actually reach up to place a hand over my chest as bright white lights shine behind me and then disappear.

"How long?"

"The entire time. Did you think I'd risk anything happening to you?"

Gratitude is a strange thing. Sometimes it feels warm and hugs every inch of you. Sometimes it strangles you and makes you feel rotten and unworthy. The latter is what I struggle with as Jase continues to tell me what to do.

Follow Seth to a hotel.

Stay there tonight.

Meet Jase tomorrow for dinner.

He ends the rattled-off list of things I'm required to do with, "We need to have a conversation."

The pit of my stomach sinks as I take in my current reality.

"I was a fool to think I'd outrun you, wasn't I?" My

words are whispered and as they leave me, Seth's car comes to life. As he pulls up in front of my house, his eyes meet mine in the faint darkness. I rip my gaze away.

"You're far from a fool, but running from me ... it won't be tolerated, Miss Fawn."

CHAPTER 4

Bethany

THERE'S A SAYING ABOUT LIFE AND HOW IT can be anything you want it to be. I forget how it goes exactly. Not that it matters, because the saying is a fucking lie. You can't just decide one day you're going to change and everything will change with you. That's not how it works. That's not life. It's more complicated than that.

Life is a tangled mess of other people's bullshit and other people's decisions. Even decisions they make on a whim.

Sometimes, you get to decide whether or not you care about them and their issues. If you do, you're fucked. Their problems become yours and sometimes that means you fall down a black hole and there's no easy escape. "Today I choose to be happy," is a joke. You can't be happy when there's a rope around your neck and another around your feet. You can't step forward, and even if you could, you'd just hang yourself.

Sometimes you don't get to decide a damn thing at all. There's not a choice you could have made that would have prevented what's to come. My sorry ass has been thinking about that all day. Whether I had a choice or not. And if what I choose is what I deserve.

Because right now it feels like that rope is pulled snug under my chin with another wrapped tight around my ankles, scratching against my skin with every step I take.

As I stare at the slip of paper I've kept in my wallet that says, *in a life where you can be anything, be kind*, I don't think twice about balling it up to toss the crumpled scrap in the trash can outside the restaurant.

I miss on the first try. *Figures.* It mocks me as it falls to the ground, daring me to pick it up and really discard it. Which I do, albeit spitefully.

A strong gust of wind blows the hair from out of my face, and without the scarf I left in my car, the chill sweeps down my collarbone and seeps into my jacket. The weather is just as bitter as I am.

I don't know how long I've been standing outside of Crescent Inn, one of the nicer restaurants in this town. I've always wanted to come here, but I could never justify it because of the price. Pulling my coat collar tighter around myself I peek in through the large floor-to-ceiling windows, past the wooden blinds that only cover the top third of the windows and search for Jase.

He's not hard to find. In the center of the room, filled with bright white tablecloths amid a sea of small cobalt blue vases, each housing an array of fresh flowers next to tea lights for ambience, he stands out.

Just seeing him does something to me. Even as a couple passes around me, giving me a disconcerted look for blocking the door and staring inside the place, I can't bring myself to go to him. I couldn't sleep without dreaming about him.

I can't think without wanting to know what *he* thinks about it all.

It's only when he brings his gaze to meet mine, as if he could feel my stare, that I dare consider taking the necessary steps toward him.

How did I get in this deep? How did I let the ropes of his life and my sister's death wrap so tightly around my every waking moment?

More importantly, *how the hell do I get out of this?*

I tell myself the only reason I came is because he said he found my things they stole when he called this morning. They were all thrown in a trash can a few blocks down from my place. There's no way it was a break-in. Jase is on my side; it was staged to disguise something else.

It's easier to enter though, knowing I'll get my book back.

"Good evening, Miss Fawn." The host greets me the moment I walk in. Without another word, he graciously takes my coat from me, ignoring the shock and apprehension that must show on my expression. With my jaw dropped, and the air absent from my lungs, I don't have a chance to ask him how he knew my name, as if the answer isn't obvious.

"Mr. Cross is right this way. Follow me, please." The

skin around the man's light blue eyes crinkles when he offers me a gentle smile. His suit is perfectly fitted to his proportions; his shoes are shined so well the chandeliers in the foyer of the restaurant sparkle against the black leather.

He's professional and kind. Still, I don't move. I stay where I am, knowing with every step I take that Jase Cross tells me to take, those ropes get tighter and tighter. Holding me right where he wants me.

The only saving grace is that if I don't think about it, if I just surrender to him… it will feel weightless, easy and deliciously thrilling while it lasts. If only I could think of anything but the demise of what my life once was.

The polite smile falters on the gentleman's face, emphasizing the lines around his eyes even more. The chatter of the crowded restaurant is what breaks me in this moment. There are plenty of people here, witnesses if anything were to happen. And I do need The Coverless Book. I need to know what Jenny said.

With her in mind, one imaginary rope around my ankle loosens. I'm all too aware that it belongs to her.

With every step I take, I think back to what's led me here:

Jenny's disappearance and how I couldn't let it go.
Jase's bar and how I couldn't keep my mouth shut.
Jenny's death and how I need to have justice.
The gun Jenny gave me and how I shot at Jase rather than playing dumb.
The contract I signed giving away my time and body in exchange for a debt.
And the break-in I don't know enough about. The book and the message inside I have to obtain.

They may have left the ropes for me to take, but I damn sure slipped them into place myself.

The host pulls the chair out for me as Jase stands, buttoning his jacket and pinning his gaze on me. A gaze I return.

"Thank you." My words are soft and I'm not certain if the host heard me or not, but I'm well aware that my hand is trembling as I reach for the water. Even more certain when the ice clinks against the edge of the pristine goblet.

I can tremble as much as I need. I'm in this mess of tangled lies and secrets, the violence and the need for vengeance. Even if it ends up killing me, I would have taken every step just the same if I had to do it all over again.

"You didn't sleep." Jase speaks first and I shake my head, staring at the cold drops of water that drip down the goblet as I set it on the table.

When I lift my tired eyes to his dark gaze, I answer him, "Maybe an hour. I was in and out." I swallow and place my hands in my lap before continuing. "Just couldn't stop thinking about everything."

He nods once and doesn't speak; instead he searches my expression for answers. Or maybe for where my boundaries lie with him today.

"What you did yesterday is unacceptable."

The tremors inside of me tense with irritation. "Which part exactly?" I question and the defiance is clear in my tone.

"The part where you ran from me."

"Who are you to me where that is unacceptable?"

His fixed stare narrows. "Your lover."

"Do all of your lovers owe you thousands of dollars?"

I dare to question him, feeling the anger simmer from his taut skin. It's so much easier to be angry. It's easier to yell than listen. Easier to hate what's happened, than to suffer through the aftermath.

The muscles in Jase's shoulders tighten, making him look all the more dominant and I don't stop pushing him. Maybe I have a death wish. "You're a man who coerced me, a man I fell for when we both know we shouldn't be together. And whatever's between us will end when the debt is paid. I will not listen to your every command because you happen to give one to me. If I don't want to be with you... I won't." His chest rises and falls quicker as his jaw clenches at my final words. "You'd be wise to remember I am not interested in being told what to do. This agreement was for information. That is all I want from you."

Thump, my heart wrenches inside of me knowing it's a lie. All I can do is remember CROSS in the hidden message of The Coverless Book and it stops its furious beating, but the beat it gives me in return is dulled and muted, slowing more and more by the second.

"I've already told you, I don't like it when you lie to me." He hardens his voice further as he adds, "Knock off your bullshit." Jase speaks through clenched teeth and before I can answer, a waitress appears with a bottle of wine draped with a white cloth napkin in an ice bucket and two glasses. It's a dark red with a silver label although I can't read what the label says.

I could use a glass of dark red wine. Then a long nap. One that lasts forever and takes me somewhere far away from the hell my life's become.

"Drink," he commands me when the waitress leaves

and I smirk at him.

"If you thought I wasn't going to drink, you're just as much of a fool as I am." Some spiteful side of me wants to deny the wine, just because he told me to drink it. But fuck that. It's the only good thing I have going for me.

I take a sip and time passes with neither of us saying anything. The first breath is tense, but the next comes easier. With every second that passes, the hate and anger wane, leaving only raw ugly feelings to fester inside of me. When that happens, I don't want to think. That's my harsh reality. I'd rather get lost in him when I don't have the anger to hide behind anymore.

"What changed?" he asks casually, breaking the silence.

"I don't trust you," I reply, and my answer slips out just as easily. An anxiousness wells up inside of me. I didn't mean to say it out loud. He doesn't know about the message in the book. That's really what changed although without it, I can't even say for sure what it says. The table jostles as I plant my elbow and rest my forehead in my hand while I refuse to look at him. I can't look him in the eyes; I can't take this shit. A moment passes and another.

"Is there anything you do trust about me?" he asks, not bothering to question why it is I don't trust him. Maybe he has his own reasons.

Peeking past my hand and then lowering it altogether, I answer honestly again, only this time it's a conscious decision. "I don't think you'd hurt me. Not physically... which is truly ironic considering how we met."

Only after I answer do I look into his eyes. And I see turmoil raging within them.

A SINGLE KISS

"I would never hurt you. Not in any way if I can help it."

"And what if you can't?" I ask him with the sorrow that's buried its way into my every thought finally showing. "What if there's no way for me to come out of this undamaged?"

"That's what you're afraid of? That's what you don't trust?" he questions.

I hadn't expected to be so transparent with him. I don't even think I was cognizant of what I'd said until the words were spoken. I could blame it on the lack of sleep or the wine. But a part of me wants him to take it all away. A part of me thinks he can make me believe he'll fix my problems. I don't even care that he can't. I just want to believe that he can for a moment. Just a single moment of peace. That part of me is so tired of fighting. I hate that part of me.

"I'm scared in general, Mr. Cross." Emotions tickle up my throat, but with a short clearing of my throat, they're gone. "I've found myself deeper and deeper in a hole that I don't know I'll be able to get out of." My eyes feel heavy, as does the weight against my chest.

I don't know how I'm still sitting upright at this point. That's the truth.

"The debt? Is that what you mean by the hole?" he asks although the look in his eyes tells me he knows that's not what I'm talking about. I shake my head, no, confirming his assumption.

"It's because of the break-in?" he asks and I don't answer, swallowing down the half truth and hating that it's all I'm willing to give him. "Bethany?" he presses and I finally speak, "Yes."

It's a lie though. Things changed before it. "Do you have my book?" I ask him the second I think of The Coverless Book. Seeing the underlined words in my mind and needing to read the hidden message. Clearing my throat again, I ask, "Did they find it?"

I don't know where to go from here until I know what my sister left for me.

I don't know what to think of Jase until I see what my sister said. That's what hurts the most.

Leaning back into his chair, he lets out a long exhale, staring into my eyes and not answering. His thumb rubs circles over the pad of his pointer finger and he leaves me waiting.

"Jase, please," I plead with him, seeking sympathy and mercy. "I just want the book back."

He leaves me without an answer still, but only for a moment.

Wordlessly, he raises his hand and I expect the waitress to come, but instead Seth walks forward. I hadn't seen him before this, not since last night when he brought me a duffle bag of the things I asked him to bring. With my head buried in the hotel pillow, he opened the door and left my bags for me. I barely even got to see him before he left, muttering a thank you into the pillow as the door was already closing.

He's quiet and businesslike, but he gives me a soft smile every time. He's like a warden with sympathy for his prisoner. The thought makes a sarcastic huff of a laugh leave me, although it's barely heard.

I don't know where he was hiding or if he was seated, perhaps standing. I have no idea. But Seth nods at me with the same polite smile the host had for me in the foyer. As if no one in this world would dare admit what a shit-show my life is and how I look the part for it right now.

I can't hear Jase's murmur but I don't need to. Seth disappears for a moment, swiftly walking away when the waitress arrives with oysters Rockefeller and seared scallops. Setting the large plates in the center of our table, she then places two small plates equipped with tiny seafood forks as well in front of each of us.

She's courteous and polite, smiling at me but more so at Jase before asking if we need anything else. Jase shakes his head once and I do the same, not trusting myself to speak.

"I chose the courses while waiting for you," he explains.

"I'm not hungry," I tell Jase, spotting Seth making his way back to us with The Coverless Book in his right hand by his side.

"You haven't slept; you should at least eat."

The tight smile graces Seth's lips once again and then holding out the book for me to take, he tells me, "The rest is now in your car, Miss Fawn."

"Thank you," I say, and somehow the words are spoken; how? I don't know. My head feels dizzy as I hold the book tighter than I've held anything in my life. It could give me the answers to everything.

"That's all," Jase says lowly and Seth is gone before I can say anything else. Before I can even swallow down the ball of dread that's cutting off the oxygen in my throat.

I should ask him where he found it; I should say

something or attempt to carry on conversation so it's not obvious that this book may change the way I think about him. He has no idea and he's given it over to me freely. I should try to keep my cover, but I'm an awful liar.

"I have to go to the restroom," I tell Jase as I stand up from the table and reach for my purse, setting the book inside before slinging the bag over my shoulder.

Jase only nods. I have to grip the back of my chair, taking him in for what could be the last time. The air changes around me, it moves around him, pulling me toward him, begging me to stay there... *just in case.*

I think if I ran, which I know very well I may do depending on what's in the book, I'd miss the way he looks at me the most. He doesn't just glance at me, he doesn't observe me the way others do, inconsequentially and only with little curiosity. He stares at me with a hunger and a need for more, to see more of me and what's inside of me. He looks at me like he never wants to stop seeing me.

Even knowing he's angry with me and how we're surrounded by prying eyes in a crowded restaurant, he only sees me. Yes, that's the way he looks at me. Like I'm the only one worth seeing. With my back turned to him, I know it might be the last time, and it hurts. I wasn't expecting that. I should stop expecting anything at all.

As I'm walking away, I feel the vibrations of my phone ringing silently, but I ignore it, quickening my pace to get away from Jase and from these thoughts.

The women's restroom door pushes open easily and I don't hesitate to lock myself inside of the stall farthest from the entrance, dropping my purse to the floor and quickly opening the book to where I was.

I check my phone just before opening the book, and it says Rockford called. For a second I hesitate, wondering what work wanted and why they called.

I drop it back into the inside pocket when I hear the door open and someone walking in. I can just barely make out a pair of red heels by the sink and I hear the telltale zip of a bag as she stands there. Maybe she's reapplying lipstick or checking her appearance. I have no idea, but either way, alone in the stall, I open the pages of the book, searching for the last page I read.

My eyes are tired and the black and white is more blurred than it should be. But the underlined words are still there and just beneath the lines, the first letter of the sentences are just as I remembered.

C starts the first sentence. R is next. Followed by O, S, S.

My fingertips slide against the indented lines. When Jenny left this message, I can only imagine the fear she must have felt, hiding it so deeply in this book.

With a deep, but staggering breath, I dig in my purse for a small Post-it note and a pen.

The next letter is an I. I write it down, then search for the next. M. M. I stop at the P for "Promise me you'll never leave." MMP makes no sense.

CROSSIMMP. Rubbing under my eyes and double-checking them, that's right. But it makes no sense. With my brows knit and the adrenaline pumping harder, I keep going. Q in "Quite the way to lead life." S for "Secrets always come out."

It makes no sense at all. There are no other words that can be made from the jumbled mess of letters. I search another chapter and another. Not reading at all, just gathering letters. And there's nothing else. No other words hidden.

My blood cools and I struggle not to cry.

There is no message.

Deep breath. Deep breath. Don't cry. Crying is useless.

A snide voice in the back of my head reminds me, so is searching for messages from the dead. They're gone. They don't come back. And they have nothing new to tell you.

I swear I can hear the crack that splits down my chest, through my heart and onward.

Hope is a long way of saying goodbye.

My own voice echoes in my head. Mocking some of the last words I ever spoke to my sister. And that's the moment I break down entirely. I suppose I can take the death, the coercion, the break-in, the fear of losing my life. But losing hope?

Even I can't live without hope.

So I read the lines again and again, although this time, they're blurry.

There is nothing here but false hope and lines from an old book with no title. Lines that for the life of me, my addict of a sister thought worthy of underlining, though I can't imagine why.

However gentle the knock at the stall door is, it still startles me.

Hiding my sniffling with the sound of pulling on the roll of toilet paper, I respond, "Just a minute."

"Are you all right?" The question comes out hesitantly.

"I just… is there anything I can do?"

How sweet a stranger can be. Kind and caring for someone they don't know. If she knew, she'd stay far away from me. Everyone in my life dies tragically.

"Just allergies. I'll be fine."

She stands there a second longer until I add, "Thank you though. That's very sweet of you."

"I haven't heard someone use allergies before," the stranger in dark red heels replies, letting me know she's well aware of my lies. "Is there anyone you'd like me to get for you?"

Although I owe this woman no explanation, I answer her. "No, I promise I'm fine. Just a really rough… month." I say that without thinking, because my mind is riddled with thoughts of Jenny. And how I wish this stranger could simply go get her for me.

If only it were possible. That's what I really want and need, far more than I should.

The woman leaves and another enters. I sit there for longer than I'd planned, drying my eyes and rearranging my bag before heading to the sink. There isn't a lipstick in the world that could make me look better. But I try to hide my crying with the stick of concealer and powder in my bag. And then a coat of pale pink lipstick.

Letting it all sink in, the only relief I have is that there was no message about Jase or his brothers. There is no warning to stay away from him.

That knowledge releases the only inhibition I had for not losing myself in him. What a way to mourn. Grief is an aphrodisiac, or so I've been told. Although I've done damage the last twenty-four hours and I don't know where we stand.

With my purse on my shoulder and the book safely tucked inside, I head back to the table feeling flushed, overwhelmed and with no appetite at all.

"So you weren't tunneling an escape after all," Jase jokes weakly as I sit down across from him. He sets his hand palm up on the table, but I don't reach for it.

"I was… just realized it would take a little longer than I'd like," I joke back, just as weakly. "No appetite?" I question, noting that he hasn't touched the appetizers.

He shakes his head in response, his eyes ever searching, ever wondering what I'm thinking. "I need an answer first."

"An answer to what?" I ask.

"I need you to agree to stay with me."

"No." My answer is immediate and I question my sanity. He could protect me. Jase Cross could do that. At the cost of losing my only sanctuary and the place that houses the memories I have. Living in fear is the worst thing I could agree to. I refuse to do it. I refuse to choose staying with him because I'm scared.

Angling the small fork to ease the oyster from its hold on the shell, I struggle for an excuse and the only one I can offer him. Thinking eating will appease him, I lift the oyster up so he knows I'll do just that but first I tell him, "I'd like to stay with my friend for the time being."

With a salty bite left in my mouth, I swallow the heavenly oyster and set the empty shell back down on the bed of ice. The tension doesn't wane, not even when I eat another, refusing to look Jase in the eyes.

"Don't do this," he warns me.

My gaze flicks to his. "Do what?"

"Don't make this harder. I don't understand what's gotten into you. But you should consider your options carefully."

"Is that a threat, Mr. Cross?"

Exasperation grows in his expression as he tells me his patience is wearing thin.

"What changed?" he finally asks. "You treat me like I'm an enemy and I'm starting to think I am to you now."

Thump. My heart is a treacherous bastard, begging me to tell him about the book. Begging me not to lie. Telling me he'll understand.

He pushes the issue, asking, "Is there something you're not telling me?"

Thump.

"You wanted me, and I wanted you. I thought that's where we were."

"Did you forget the other night?" I ask meekly, remembering crying in the bedroom, remembering him walking away because I couldn't admit it out loud like he has just now. Raising my eyes to him and staring back with nothing but sincerity I remind him, "It's not like the two of us should be together."

"Do you want me?" he asks, not letting anything change in his expression.

With a single hard swallow, I answer him with raw truth, "Yes. More than anything else."

"Nothing else matters then."

"Not the debt? Not the fact that someone's after me?" I feel my expression fall, the kind of crumpling that comes with an ugly cry, but I don't give a shit, I let it out, I let it all out. "Not the fact that a part of me hates you because I hate what you do and that the life you lead is why my sister's dead?" I'll never be able to say those words without tears flooding my eyes. I don't blink and a few tears fall, but I won't cry after that. Crying does nothing.

As I'm angrily wiping my tears away, I note his lack of a response and continue the onslaught. I ask him, "How much is it that I owe you again?"

"I'm fucking tired of you asking me that. It'll be months before you've paid the debt."

"*The* debt..." I whisper, sniffling and looking away thinking about how it's *her* debt, not mine. But the thoughts vanish as I note how the restaurant is slowly thinning in attendance. It's sobering, the sight around us.

It's not just thinning, everyone is leaving. There are only two couples left. And both are preparing to exit. The young woman glances at me as she pushes her chair in, her eyes wide with worry.

"Jase." I can only whisper his name as my pulse races with concern.

"I was wondering how long it would take you to notice."

Thump. Thump. Thump. It's like a war drum. I whisper the question, "What did you do?"

Leaning forward, he places his forearms on the table. His eyes darken as they sear into me. "I've let you get away with too much."

I can't breathe, and I can't move; even when I hear the door click loudly behind me and bringing with it utter silence, I don't dare to do anything but stare into his eyes.

They contain a mix of hunger and depravity. His hard

jawline tightens as he clenches his teeth and lets his eyes roam down the front of me then back to my apprehensive gaze.

"They couldn't stay here any longer, because I need to punish you. You've known this was coming. I should have done it sooner." Frustration and regret ring clear in his voice and guilt overrides my other emotions. "I take responsibility. You wouldn't behave this way if I'd punished you like I should have."

The way he says punish evokes a mix of reactions from me. I heat with desire and longing, wanting him to take control so I can stop thinking, stop doing, and just obey and receive what he's willing to give. The other reaction though comes from the knowledge of who this man is and how it will never change. Fear is ever present when he takes control.

"There are consequences. And like I've said, you've gotten away with too much."

CHAPTER 5

Jase

With the door securely locked, I check to make sure the blinds have been lowered, and they have. Although the front door window is visible from this table, meaning someone could see if they dared to peek, but Seth is waiting outside and he'd take care of that problem before any prick would have the chance to see a damn thing.

"Jase, I'm sorry." Bethany's voice wavers as she speaks, showing her fear. I wondered which side of her would take over. I was hoping it wouldn't be this one. It makes everything more difficult, but she must be punished. This has to stop.

"You aren't. If you were sorry, you wouldn't continue to defy me." A deep inhale barely keeps me grounded as my temper flares. "You are the only one who has ever made me lose control like this. Do you know that?"

"Jase, I don't mean to," she nearly whimpers with more than a hint of fear and finally glances away from me, toward the door.

Her breathing is erratic and her fingers wrap around her silverware as if she'll use it against me. She may do just that, my fiery girl, if I give her a reason.

"Jase," she says and whispers my name.

"You're scared?" I ask her.

She hesitates to answer before closing her eyes and nodding. The fear is a constant. I'm not sure it'll ever leave her and I can't blame her.

"You just said you trusted that I would never hurt you." The pain inside of my chest is sharp like a knife, piercing and twisting, never stopping to offer a moment of relief. I'd bleed out here if I had to watch her paused in this moment, truly afraid that I'd hurt her. "I'm not going to hurt you, Bethany. This is a punishment that you can take. One that you obviously need."

"I'm scared," she whispers.

"Don't be. Parts of it you may even enjoy." That comment gets her attention. I keep her gaze to tell her, "I'm not going to let you get away with this shit any longer. You will be punished. Whether you're upset or scared or otherwise. I should have already punished you." At the word punish, she licks her lips. Her body will always betray her regardless of the brave front she puts on around me.

"You've run from me, lied to me, stolen from me, raised a knife to me… And you thought I'd do nothing?" I question her. "How much did you think I'd let you get away with, cailín tine?"

Using her nickname is what does it. I can feel the tension break, I can feel it warm and I notice how it melts around her. Her bottom lip drops, pouty and trembling, but her breathing has changed. No longer tense, but still quick with anticipation.

I give her a moment, letting everything settle for her.

"Still your cailín tine?" The Gaelic phrase sounds foreign on her tongue.

"Of course," I answer, reaching across the table to offer my hand and she still hesitates to reciprocate, but she does, setting her small hand in mine. Brushing my thumb across her wrist, I try to keep it soothing to calm her before the inevitable will happen. "I hate that it comes to this before you'll let me in. Do you know that?"

She exhales deeply before telling me, "I'm not exactly used to this. And I don't exactly like it either."

"You don't like what?"

"Having to be accountable to someone like…"

"To someone like me?" She only nods at my question until I narrow my gaze and pause the motion of my thumb against her pulse. "Yes," she answers verbally.

"Well I enjoy your company, Miss Fawn, and from what I gather, you enjoy mine." Again she nods and this time whispers her yes along with it, nearly defiantly.

"When you're with someone, you have to make allowances for them. I have done my best to make allowances for you given this… situation."

"And I have not," Beth speaks before the judgment can fall from my lips. "I realize I am difficult and…" she pauses, swallowing thickly before adding, "I do appreciate some things… I am just very aware of others that…"

"That you will have to make certain allowances for," I say, finishing her sentence for her with the only outcome I'll allow. "Is that understood?"

She nods and speaks simultaneously, "Yes."

Pulling my hand away from her, I let the warmth of her words—that she appreciates me, no matter how small a part of me— flow through me, feeling my cock harden as I think about what I'm going to do to her. "This situation being new for you is no excuse. It's new for me too."

"What are you going to do?" she asks breathlessly.

"You're going to need the rest of your wine."

I'm careful and calm as I stand up, pulling the chair back and unbuttoning my jacket.

Her fingers linger on the glass but she doesn't pick it up until I pick up my own glass, downing the full-bodied red I know she loves. It's sweet and decadent, like her when she lets go and gives me control.

I set the empty glass on the table behind us. The aftertaste is smooth and I focus on that as I calmly remove everything from our table one by one. The candle, the vase, the small plates and then the large one still littered with hors d'oeuvres I thought she'd enjoy.

She doesn't just calm down; that wouldn't fit the woman she is. She's intense and wrought with emotion. She feels everything in exaggerated stages.

Every second that passes, the air gets hotter around us.

Each breath she takes picks up its pace.

After loosening my tie, I remove the last few pieces of silverware from the table, placing it easily on the table to our right.

"Sit here." My hand splays on the barren table in front

of me. My palm is flat against the surface. "Right here," I say and pat the table again, closer to the edge this time and although she's slow, she obeys. Climbing onto the table, she's fully clothed. The blush that creeps up her cheeks is an indication that she knows damn well she won't be staying that way.

"Come closer," I command once she's on all fours on top of the table and when she's close enough, I position her body how I want it, feeling the race of adrenaline and desire run through my pulse.

"Jase." My name is merely lust wrapped in words that don't matter. "I really am sorry."

"I have a question for you," I say, and I don't bother accepting or denying her apology. "Are you terrified of me? Or of what I could do to you?" I ask her, placing my forearms on the table on either side of her. She's close to me, her luscious curves within reach. Her pouty lips near mine, ready to capture. But I don't kiss her. Not yet.

"Both," she admits and I don't blame her.

"I've done terrible things in my life. It makes sense you'd be afraid," I admit, feeling a crease in my forehead as her expression stays etched with concern. "But leading with fear is a bad move to make."

"I know," she whispers just beneath her breath. "I don't know what I'm doing. I don't know what I've gotten myself into. I'm angry, I'm lost and I'm terrified."

"I'll be angry alongside you. I'll find you a way. I'll make sure there's not a damn thing that will touch you. Nothing should scare you when you're with me." Reaching out, I cup her chin in my hand, feeling her smooth skin and continuing to caress her when she presses her cheek into my embrace. "Even me. I shouldn't scare you."

"Knowing how much I want to be around you is terrifying in itself. Which is ridiculous, all things considered." Her eyes open on her last point, her thick lashes barely revealing her eyes beneath them.

With one leg on either side of me, I press my fingers against her pussy, through the fabric that separates our skin and she keeps her eyes on mine, but her head falls back just slightly.

"Already hot," I comment. "Are you already wet for me too?"

She only nods and as I open my lips, moving closer to her to reprimand her for not answering verbally, she halts any inclination I have to do so.

She kisses me first. Without warning. Surprised, I moan into her mouth, feeling my rigid cock twitch with need to be inside of her. This greedy woman who takes from me when no one else would dare to do so.

"Even when you're in trouble, you still defy me and take from me."

She only answers with the hint of smile.

"You like to be the first to kiss, don't you?" I ask her.

"It's my call." I don't bother to hide the smirk that lurks on my lips.

I don't bother to hide the lust either as I answer her, "It was going to happen anyway."

"I could have run, I could bite you, or deny you."

"Why would you?" I ask her with genuine curiosity, my lips just barely away from hers.

"That's what people do when they're scared, Jase. You should know that by now."

Words catch in my throat, tightening it and warring with each other inside of me. "Strip" is the only one that manages to escape.

"Jase." I watch her swallow, I can even hear it before she tells me, "They'll see. Anyone could see from the door."

"I don't give a shit about anyone but you right now."

Words are lost to her as we stare into each other's eyes until I tell her, "Any man who dared to look through that door would die."

Her breath hitches and her thighs tighten at my words.

"Does that make you hot?" I ask her, feeling my own desire rising.

She nods as she whispers yes. I allow my gaze to wander down her body, although it stops too soon as I focus on her breasts when she pulls her sweater over her head. Through the tank top underneath, I see her pebbled nipples.

"Maybe he'd get a glimpse of you cumming with my lips between your legs."

Leaning in closer, I whisper in her ear as she pulls the straps of her tank top down, "What a way to die… for that to be the last thing he sees."

The exhale she releases is tempting, but I maintain control. I don't touch her again as she peels off every bit of clothing and lies bared to me, pushing her bra off the table for it to fall carelessly on the floor below with its companions.

Both of my hands grip her hips and I pull her closer to me. Keeping her gaze with mine, I lower my lips to her swollen nub and suck. With a single lick of her sweet cunt, I go back to her clit, sucking it until she's letting those sweet sounds flow into the air.

Her body rocks, her hands spear my hair. I love the way her nails scratch me as she gets closer and closer.

I have to remind myself that this is a punishment. I can't get lost in her.

The moment her back arches and her bottom lip drops with a deep moan, I pull away from her, smacking the inside of her thigh to take her away from the edge of her forbidden fall.

"No," I tell her. With flushed cheeks, she stares back at me breathlessly and wordlessly. "You don't get to cum tonight."

As she blinks away the haze of lust and confusion, my middle finger plays at her folds, spreading her arousal as I talk. "I will play with you, fuck you, and get myself off with the things I plan to do with you. But you will not cum."

All I can hear is her single breath before she nods.

"Verbally."

"I understand."

Rewarding how easily she accepts the punishment, I plant a kiss on the bright red patch of skin on her inner thigh. And then another, traveling up her body, over the curve of her waist and then higher. Standing up and dragging my open-mouth kisses up her neck, I unbutton my pants, letting them and my boxers drop to the floor so I can stroke myself.

"On your back," I command her and pull my shirt over my head. She positions herself with her heels on the edge of the table and her back flat against the tabletop.

She struggles not to lift her head and watch me as I undress entirely.

I can't resist toying with her breasts, plucking her nipples and pulling them back to bring those sweet sounds to leave her.

Her pussy clenches around nothing. I watch her, hot and flushed, ready to be fucked. The taste of her and red wine still remain on my tongue.

"You're taking this punishment well," I commend her and then pull her ass closer to me, nearly falling off the edge of the table.

She starts to answer, but I grip her hips in my hand and slam myself inside her. Fuck, she feels too fucking good. I can't close my eyes even though my body begs me to enjoy the rapture of pleasure fully and do so.

Her neck arches and her eyes scrunch as her heat clenches around me. The table jostles with the thrust of my hips and her breasts sway as I fuck her. I'm careful not to allow her to enjoy herself fully.

Her hands move to her breasts, her nipples barely peeking through her fingers as she gets close, inching her way toward her release.

I pull out fully, instantly missing her warmth.

She whimpers and struggles to stay still as I step back. It's hard to keep my breathing controlled, even harder to do it again, fucking her relentlessly on the table and stopping just before she reaches her climax.

The third time, I lower my body close to hers, feeling my skin heat and needing to be closer to her. She doesn't kiss me when I bring my lips close to hers this time.

She pushes her head back against the table, so I drag my teeth along her throat and up to the shell of her ear, loving how she moans even though she knows she'll be left wanting yet again.

"This is what a punishing fuck is," I hiss as I pound into her again and stay buried deep inside of her as I almost lose myself in the moment. "I take all my pleasure," I push the words through clenched teeth as I move myself slowly out of her and then slam all the way back in.

A strangled cry leaves her and she drags her nails down my back. The mix of pleasure and pain nearly has me finding my release too soon. I'm not ready for it to be over though, not by a mile.

"I get my pleasure, and you get nothing," I whisper in her ear as the intensity of the pleasure stirring inside of me subsides. Only then am I able to pull away from her enough to look her in the eye.

Daggers stare back at me, but not in anger. I can see the challenge clearly written on her face. My poor cailín tine has no idea how painful orgasm denial is. To be taken to the highest high each time, finding the edge of release so close, only to have it ripped away from you and the waves of pleasure yanked from you.

"I dream about the noises you make when you get off. I want to hear those sounds over and over again," I tell her and then recklessly fuck her, feeling the stir of my climax approaching in time with hers. Only to pull away at the last second.

"No," this time she whimpers and her body rolls to the side, wanting to get away. "Please," she begs me, her face pained.

"How can I reward either of us with that, when you don't listen to me? When you fight me every step of the way?"

She visibly swallows and tells me she's sorry again. I'm not interested in an apology.

I fuck her again, listening to the sound of me fucking her, of the table banging against the floor as my movements get stronger with my own needs taking over.

I suck in a deep breath as I pull away again. She can't resist touching herself, knowing it's only a small touch she'll need at this point and I grip her wrists, pulling them away and pinning them to the table.

The frustration, even the contempt, show in her expression. "Keep your hands here." My voice is deep and the threat is there. I can tell she's biting her tongue and I love it. I love taming my wild girl.

"Let me be very clear. I would have loved to get lost inside of you and give you every pleasure imaginable. But I will not be made a fool, Bethany. Do you understand?"

"I'm not a fucking idiot."

"You put a knife against my chest," I rebut. "That doesn't make you a smart woman, does it?"

"I'm sorry," she tells me again and her gaze falls to my chest, but I grip her chin, stealing her attention back to what matters.

"Do you think words are enough? Words are meaningless."

She shakes her head. "I can't go back. What more do you want from me?" She screams her question, the hoarse words ricocheting in the restaurant.

Even now she pushes me. She'll never stop. I know she won't. The fire inside of her will never die.

And I love it. I will live for the moments she defies me.

Knowing that to be the truth, I pin her hands above

her head when I thrust inside of her this time and push my chest to hers. My muscles scream and a cold sweat breaks out along my back as I rut between her legs, hard and deep, listening to her strangled cries of pleasure.

I nearly don't stop. I nearly ruin the punishment, but fate would have me go through with it. The leg of the table that's closest to me, buckles and breaks. Forcing us to fall as the table crashes to the floor.

Silencing her scream with a desperate kiss, I pull her body on top of mine as my back falls against the broken wood. With an arm wrapped around her back, I roll over to lay her on the floor.

I only take a moment to make sure she's all right, and her response is to writhe under me, begging me to keep fucking her.

I slam myself as hard and deep as I can inside of her and stay right there. She claws at the floor, screaming and moaning with nothing to silence her cries.

Watching her gasp for air and struggling to contain herself, I push the question out with what little control I have left. "Tell me what you really think of me."

I shouldn't have asked and it shouldn't matter, but in this moment, being inside of her and having her at my mercy, I need to know. More than anything else, I need to know the truth.

She struggles not to thrash under me as I rub her clit, still buried inside of her. "Tell me the truth, cailín tine."

"I love you," she practically screams the repressed truth and I still. My body tenses, even as she continues to thrash beneath me, heaving in air and still pushing me away, although weakly.

I have to move. Before I lose myself inside her, and before she says anything else.

She loves me.

I fuck her with long strokes, each of them penetrating her as deeply as I can and pulling out until I'm barely inside of her.

Each time she lets out a moan of sudden pleasure and then her eyes seek mine, wanting more, needing me again and again.

I draw out her release, teasing her like this and nipping her lips. All the while hearing her say those words over and over in my head. *She loves me.*

She whispers it again, right when her pussy tightens and she cries out her orgasm.

When I finally feel my own release, I sink my teeth into her neck, not biting her, but needing to do something so I don't groan out words I'll regret.

The haze of desire fades slowly and then all at once when I sit up, pulling myself away from her, and she finally looks me in the eyes.

For a long time, the only thing I can hear is both of us breathing, both of us getting a grip on what just happened. She said she loves me.

As I clean between her legs, pressing the cloth napkin against her clit and forcing her head to fall back from the pressure, I'm all too aware that I didn't say the words back.

And I don't plan on it.

"You're not going to your friend's house to put her in danger and you're not going to a fucking hotel and leaving my men out there to watch over you. You're coming home with me."

A SINGLE KISS

Shock colors her expression at first when I stand up and leave her where she is. She reaches for her tank top before anything else and then finally looks up at me.

"I don't love you." The words rush out of her, the hurt written on her face. She tries to swallow up the evidence of her lie, but it doesn't work.

"Of course you don't," is all I answer her, burying the sensation that grows inside of me. I turn my back to her while putting my pants back on as she cleans herself up. "You're coming home with me," I repeat, focusing on what matters. A truth she can't deny, unlike what she's doing now.

The chair behind me groans against the floor as it's moved and I peek over my shoulder to see her nearly dressed and avoiding eye contact. "Did you hear me?" I ask her, feeling something stir inside my chest with restlessness.

Bethany kicks aside a scrap of wood to stand and nods her head while answering me, "Yes, and that's fine. I don't want to go back to my place anyway." Her voice is low, too low and devoid of any of the fight I'm used to from her.

The silence of the restaurant is uncanny as we wait there, with my eyes on her and her eyes anywhere else.

"Seth's waiting for us outside. You'll follow me and he'll be behind you."

She nods and audibly swallows but doesn't say anything else as she wraps her arms around one another. Not crossing her arms in front of her chest, but laying them atop each other. Her gaze lingers on the front door, but she doesn't move until I splay my hand on the small of her back.

That gets a reaction from her. She walks faster, fast enough for the pressure of my touch to be meaningless.

No one's out front of the restaurant, no one except Seth leaning against the hood of his black Audi and keeping watch. The light dusting of white on the ground outside is evidence that the snow must have come and gone already. Leaving behind it a thick white fog, and the curtain of white across every surface.

Bethany lets me open the front door for her and I'm granted a muted thank you. Same with her car door. She doesn't look toward Seth at all; she merely focuses her attention on each of her steps.

Seth's gaze turns questioning. Anyone with any common sense can see she's not well.

"Upset" is hardly a word I would use to describe Bethany. It's too weak. She's too volatile to simply be upset. But right now, it's the only word I can find. She's upset and I fucking hate it.

I love you.

She said it and then took it back. She's confused and upset. Confusion runs deep in my mind as well. For the first time since I've set eyes on her, I'm uncertain what to do with her.

I want to hear her tell me those words again, and to mean it. But I would never wish for a girl like her to fall for me, either.

"You can close the door, Mr. Cross," she tells me, staring at my shoes from where she sits in the driver's seat. The clinking of her keys is all I can hear as I stare down at her, waiting for her to look up at me. My hand is still firmly on her car door.

A gust of wind passes and I can hear Seth clear his throat in the distance. Still I don't look away, and neither does she.

"Bethany," I murmur her name and she hums back, a sweet sound, seemingly just fine, but still doesn't look at me.

"What's wrong?" My grip tightens on the door when the question leaves me. I already know and I feel like an asshole. She's a mess. That's all she's been since I've come into her life. A mess, but a beautiful masterpiece. She'll do more good in a week at the hospital than I'll do in my entire life. There's no questioning that.

"Nothing," she answers in a whisper, then peeks up at me, toying with her keys in her hand and offering a sad smile.

"You look like you're going to cry."

Her voice in response is stubborn, but it also cracks. "I'm not."

"Get out of the car, Bethany." I give her the command and step back although I keep my grip on the door, pulling it open wider and waiting on the vacant street. I can't help but notice our footprints on the sidewalk. Hers are so much smaller than mine, but the spacing is the same. They're in complete rhythm and time with mine.

She clears her throat as she steps out, moving over the curb and onto the sidewalk. Toe to toe with me, she stands there, both of her hands cradling the keys. Maybe to keep them from making noise, maybe to give her something to focus on other than me.

Either way she looks me in the eyes, daring me to accuse her of being on the verge of tears again. I can see it.

Instead I tell her, "I don't love you too." I don't think about it; I just say it. Feeling the restlessness sway inside of me, panicking and not knowing how she'll react.

Her large hazel eyes widen even more, for only a moment as her lips part just slightly and other than that, there's no response at all. No telling as to what she thinks. Until she tries to speak and the first word can't even make it out unbroken.

Instead of carrying on with the intention of speaking, she snags her bottom lip between her teeth to keep it from trembling and stares at the window of the car door rather than at me.

I add, leaning closer to her, close enough to feel her warmth and for her hair to kiss against me with the upcoming gust, "I lied to you and you lied to me. Now we're lying to each other."

I hate myself in this moment, for daring to lead her into this path. But the other path is away from me. I want her close, I need her as close to me as I can have her.

Her hazel eyes swirl with a mix of emotions. Complicated and in broken disarray, the amber colors bleeding into one another, but each still visible and adding to the beauty of her gaze.

"I don't love you." She shakes her head as the statement leaves her. Her body consciously denying the very words she speaks.

"I don't love you too," I repeat.

She's searching. Trying to figure out whether or not I'm lying to her and I don't know what she'll find. I don't know if I'm even capable of loving anymore. Not the way she needs. Not the way she deserves.

Before she can find whatever truth there is, I crash my lips against hers, letting go of the door to pull her into my arms. Her soft lips melt as I deepen the kiss. Her small hands reach up to push against my chest, but instead she quickly fists my coat and pulls me in even closer.

With a swift glide of my tongue against the seam of her lips, she parts them for me and lets me in. In the middle of the empty sidewalk, I pour everything into that kiss, holding her body against mine. Letting her feel what it is that I have. Maybe she can feel what I have for her. Maybe she'll know it better than I can.

I can feel her heart pound against her chest, maybe hating my own, maybe needing another to commiserate with.

CHAPTER 6

Bethany

The quiet is uncomfortable. Or maybe it's just my thoughts filling up the silence that are uncomfortable. Every second, I go through an entire day. Each day since Jenny's gone missing, even worse when she was found dead, and then each day that Jase tore through the shambles of my life.

That's what the mind does when placed in a quiet room.

His bedroom is a subdued masculinity. A calming presence that begs me to lie down and sink into the plush linens. But then… the thoughts come back. The memories. The what-ifs.

Sitting on the edge of his bed, I focus on the chaos that used to be. The Rockford Center kept me busy, kept me going. And I miss it.

I miss my patients. Marky Lindgren in particular. He always had a story to tell. Sometimes the patients are violent. Sometimes they're vile with what they say. Sometimes all they do is cry, and I keep reminding myself of what I'd tell them when they apologized.

"You're having a moment and you can have as many as you need."

People mourn differently. Funny how on this side of it all, I find my own advice something to ignore. I don't need moments; I need a way forward.

And that's why I miss Marky. Marky's a liar and he spins stories about the other patients to occupy his time. I remember one night he told me how the male patient at the end of the hall had slept with one of the patients that had just been admitted.

He said it so confidently, so seriously, I almost believed him.

And then he told me how she just had to break it off with her husband who was in room 3B. But the man in 3B wasn't going to let her go without a fight and that's what all the commotion was about. Why everyone was crying and yelling.

He said it was a love triangle and then he added... the man at the end of the hall would be fine with a threesome, but he'd never admit it to the woman. I shake my head remembering how he said it, baiting me and waiting for a response I didn't give him.

Each time someone would walk past his room, he'd create a dialogue on what they thought of the adulteress and the sordid affair that never took place. Some of his comments made me genuinely laugh.

The first time I let the smile show on my face, he laughed and then I with him.

He would break up the time with stories that didn't matter, stories you could get lost in. I let myself get lost in them too, because the man in 3B was always angry due to having Alzheimer's and not knowing why he was there. And the man at the end of the hall was violent because he wanted to end it all and we had to strap him down to keep him from doing just that. All over a job he'd lost. It was just a job and just an income. But the debt was too much for him to bear.

Real life didn't matter in Marky's stories though, and amid the chaos, the rounds of delivering pills and checking on patients, Marky's stories made some horrific days tolerable.

No matter how bad the days got though, going home I felt accomplished, needed, and like the chaos was worth it.

The man at the end of the hall found a way out of the hole he'd dug himself with bankruptcy. The man in 3B remembered some of the best times of his life when his family came and they'd just come two weeks ago before I was told to go on leave; it made all the difference for him.

I still don't know about the woman who just came in. She's not from around here and we were told to keep her "attendance"—as they called it—private.

I wasn't even given her full name, only initials.

I miss the chaos, I miss Marky's stories, I even miss my boss and the bullshit rotating schedule. I miss my mind being occupied.

Right now, in the quietness of Jase's bedroom, I'd prefer to be in the halls of the Rockford Center, wondering what everyone else's story is and helping them with their tales, rather than having to face my own.

A creak in the hall catches my attention. A sputtering in my chest echoes to the pit of my stomach. "Jase?" I call out when the door doesn't open.

It's his own bedroom, so if he wanted to come in, surely he would.

But the door doesn't open and I'm left staring at a doorknob I haven't dared touch and wondering what the fuck I'm doing.

Neither of us spoke last night really. Which is for the best. I don't trust the words coming out of my mouth when he's near me.

So we didn't speak, apart from the necessary details.

Half a bottle of zinfandel, a full dish of chicken parmesan, and a soft pillow in a quiet house, with the firm chest at my back of a man who says he'll keep me safe... and I fell asleep. A deep sleep, one where you don't move and you don't dream, because your body sleeps just as heavily as your mind.

That's the kind of sleep I had and then I woke up to a note from Jase, letting me know that he'd be back later tonight and to "make myself comfortable."

I've been torn and now I'm breaking down. If I were at work right now, visitors might think I should be in one of the rooms, rather than in my scrubs holding a tray of medication to dish out.

Do I love Jase? I don't know. It's easy to want love when you're hurting. It's easy to hold on to anything that could fill the void pain has caused. I don't know what's real, and what's the product of coping.

Does Jase Cross love me? No. He doesn't. Not at all.

I think he feels bad for me. It's all sympathy. The way he looked at me tonight said it all. He feels sorry for me.

It's such bullshit. But at least I'm safe. All I need to be, right now, is safe.

And that's the dichotomy I'm supposed to *make myself comfortable* in.

He left me two rules on the slip of paper as well:

If the door is locked, stay out.

Your handprint opens the front door and the hall door behind the stairwell. Don't open the hall door at the moment and don't leave. I'm trusting you.

In other words, stay right where I left you. If I didn't feel so tired, I'd have my ass out of that front door, and walk in knee-deep snow to some shady hotel I could afford. Just to spite him.

But I'm tired. All the sleep in the world can't help the type of tired I am.

You may be tired, Bethany Ann Fawn, you may be sad and in a shit position, but you are still a badass. You are not going to take any shit. And those rules Jase left you, those rules that sexy motherfucker thinks he can lay down while trapping you here, those rules can go fuck themselves.

My little pep talk kicks my lips up into a grin and the lyrics to a Pretty Reckless song play in my mind.

Tell them it's good. Tell them okay, but don't do a goddamn thing they say.

It's been my life's motto. Nothing's going to change that.

My first move is to push the curtains in the bedroom as far open as I can. They're heavy and the sky is full of white fog, not offering much light at all. I think it's the winter that's gotten me so down, at least it's part of the reason. The season can take some of this blame.

With a little more light in his too-dark-even-with-the-light-on bedroom, I go drawer by drawer. I don't find anything interesting. Socks, neatly folded in a row. Same with his ties. I let my fingers linger over them, feeling the silk and wondering how he could even choose a tie like this, given the patterns are hidden this way.

I finally find a drawer that's mostly empty; it only houses two pairs of jeans I'm able to put in his undershirt drawer, which is filled with white and black cotton undershirts... and now two pairs of jeans.

All of my things don't even fill the drawer: two pairs of PJs, a pair of sweats, a pair of jeans and a few tops. It's everything that was in my clean laundry basket. I have a closet full of clothes, but I wear these garments over and over again. What can I say? I like what I like and I damn well like to be comfortable.

The toiletries are next, but there's not a space in the medicine cabinet, nor under the sink. I'm able to clear room in the linen closet and shamelessly rearrange what was under the cabinet, putting most of it in the closet and finding a place for my own things there.

A tightness starts in my abdomen and works its way up every time I peek at the medicine cabinet. The pills are still at my house; the ones I stole from Jase. That's the only spot available to put anything in there, but I don't bother to touch anything else in that cabinet.

All in all, I waste about an hour. That's all the time I could fill. Then I'm back to staring at the doorknob, wondering when Jase will be back, wondering if I should leave, if I should go. All the wondering that drives me mad.

The clouds shift behind me, as does the faint light in the room. A band of white light shines across the room until it lands on my purse. It's only then that I realize my phone is probably dead since I haven't charged it.

As I'm rummaging for it, I take out The Coverless Book. I have no right to feel betrayed by it, but I do. Jase's charger on his nightstand works for my phone and once it comes to life, I stare at a blank screen. No missed calls and no missed texts.

I call the Center, keeping the phone plugged in and sitting on the edge of Jase's side of the bed. I'm given the voicemail before the second ring occurs. They shunted me there intentionally. If they were just going to ignore me, why bother calling yesterday?

I listen to the voicemail message far too long before hanging up. I have no one right now. No one.

The only people waiting for me, are the fictional characters in The Coverless Book.

CHAPTER 7

Jase

I COULD HARDLY FOCUS ON THE UPDATE FROM Carter this morning. Romano's planning something judging by how he's moving storage units and Carter thinks he might take off, so we have to strike now if we want a chance at getting him before he leaves. He said Officer Walsh has members of the FBI in town, something about them being involved with Romano's indictment. They're all over him and watching his every move, which makes it impossible for us to do a damn thing.

I couldn't focus on anything he was telling me in his office. All I could think about was how Bethany had wrapped her arms around me in the middle of her sleep. She clung to me without knowing, nestling her head against my chest. I could live a thousand lives in that single moment.

All I could picture was how serene she looked in her

sleep. All throughout the conversation with Carter and all throughout the drive to the club.

If she knew her sister was still alive, she wouldn't sleep like that. If she finds out I knew and I didn't tell her, she wouldn't cling to me like she had last night.

I only have one lead that could change the course of where this is all going. One chance, one moment, to hold on to Bethany like I want to. One lead, who's waiting for me just beyond the glowing red lights of the sign ahead of me.

The Red Room isn't just a cover. It's not just for laundering and meetups. Just like the storage shed behind it isn't exactly what it looks like. It's inconspicuous, large and organized with wide open spaces. Everything clearly seen on first glance when you walk into the storage shed which measures forty feet on each side. I demand it be kept clean and tidy. So anyone looking for any hint of it being anything other than a place to keep the extra bottles of liquor and tables would know at first glance there's nothing else here.

Unless they opened the safe and found the secret door in the back of it. It leads to a winding iron staircase, down to a long hall in the basement with a vault door to a room.

The skinny hallway that leads to the room reminds me of the old warehouse I'd sneak off to when I was a boy. Back when I needed to be alone and get away. It was quiet, and offered the comfort of both safety and a place to simply be alone.

The room in that basement exists for one purpose. And one purpose only.

The men who find themselves here aren't feeling

the security I did when I was younger and hiding in the warehouse.

No, the men who end up in this room are here to die, although they would say and do anything to believe that they'll get out of here still breathing.

The vault door opens with a slow, plaintive cry. It's heavy and made of thick steel. With Seth behind me, we enter the room comprised of four smooth concrete walls. It's soundproof and the floors are made of steel grids with a drain in the center of the room.

There's no furniture in the room, save an old iron chair bolted to the floor over the drain. I bring everything I need with me each time.

This time I've brought a pair of hedge clippers, the kind most people use for their gardens. They're in my back pocket, as is my pocket knife.

The muffled screams that come from behind the balled cloth in Luke Stevens's mouth fill the room as the two of us walk in.

His skin's paler and almost gray in this light than it was in the video we had of him and another man talking about where Marcus wanted Jenny Parks delivered. That's the word that came out of his mouth. Delivered. As if she were only an object to be shipped off.

The steel cuffs leave bright red marks around his wrists and ankles, along with a trail of dried blood as he wrestles with his restraints, still screaming. Like it would do him any good to fight.

My nostrils flare with the stench of piss in the damp underground as I get a few feet from him and then look to my right to ask Seth, "How long?"

"Twelve hours now."

He stands closer to the prisoner than I do. We have a system that works. When something works, you don't fuck it up. He knows that and he stands where he always does, just behind the subject of our interrogation, where he can't be seen.

Crouching in front of Luke, a man who may know where Jenny is, I look into his dark eyes, taking in how dilated they are. Wondering what the hell he's on.

"You think twelve hours is enough?" I ask Seth and he shrugs. Luke struggles to look behind him, and his ass comes off the chair just slightly, but the chain wrapped around his waist keeps him down.

Standing up straighter, I pull the clippers from my back pocket and unlock them to look at the blade. "They're dull," I comment as if I didn't notice before.

"They'll still work," Seth says and this time he places a hand on either side of the back of the chair, close enough to Luke so our victim notices, but still not touching him.

I can imagine how Luke's heart races, how the adrenaline takes over. The fight or flight response failing him and every instinct in his body screaming for him to beg. Just like he's screaming now, behind the old shirt shoved in his mouth. Seth's silent and that's how he'll stay until I ask him if there's any reason not to kill the man in the chair.

"Take it out." On my command, Seth removes the shirt from Luke's mouth, ripping the duct tape across his skin in a swift motion. The bright pink skin left behind marks where the tape once laid.

"I didn't do it," Luke screams immediately. Even as the pain tears through him and he's forced to wince, he continues to plead. "Whatever it is, I didn't do it. I didn't fuck with you guys."

"Jenny Parks," I say quietly, and it's all I say. Realization dawns on the man that he did, in fact, do it. He fucked with us. And it shuts him up, although his bottom lip still quivers.

There's a knowing look of fear in his eyes. The lack of an exhale, the stale gaze he gives me. "You know her name."

His mouth closes before he speaks and he visibly swallows.

"Every time you hesitate, I take something from you," I tell him easily, crouched in front of him and waiting for him to acknowledge what I've said.

The second his mouth opens to speak, I grip his hand, choosing his pointer first. The clank of the cuffs and his protests mix in the damp air that still smells like piss. Seth does his part, shoving the shirt in the man's mouth as I clamp down on the clippers. My left hand keeps the other fingers bent, stopping them from interfering. My right hand closes the blades around his pointer. The flesh cuts easily; blood flows just as easily as he lets out a high-pitched muffled scream, but the bone I have to break away from the ligament first before it's cleanly gone.

I take a half step back, watching the blood pour from where his finger was moments ago. It streams out steadily and more blood creeps from under the metal cuffs that keep him held down as he struggles. Seth keeps his hand over the shirt, and watches Luke's face turn bright red, struggling to breathe, screaming with everything he has in him.

His chest heaves. But it never lasts long. The screaming

is only temporary. Just like the hesitation and the lies.

"I've done this a few times, Mr. Stevens," I comment as I wipe the blade on his dark blue denim jeans. Although he's stopped screaming, the shirt stays where it is. Seth knows to only remove it once I'm ready for the man to speak.

I let out a heavy exhale and then crouch down in front of him again as I say, "I don't like to waste my time." My tone is easy, consoling even as I stare into his bloodshot eyes, noting the desperation that flows from his sweaty skin. I tell him, "I just want answers, and then all of this is over."

He tries to shriek through the shirt, his neck craning as he more than likely pleads with Seth to remove the gag. The tendons in his neck tense and he keeps it up, which only pisses me off.

"We don't have time for your comments or questions. Now answer mine. Do you know Jenny Parks?"

With the question asked, Seth removes the rag and the man in the chair stumbles over his words.

"She's the girl I took to the bridge." He does well with the first statement, but then he backtracks and barters. My irritation would show, if I weren't expecting it. After all, I have done this more than a few times. He started off strong, thinking it was a negotiation, but the tilt of my head changed his tone to one of a beggar.

"If I tell you everything… will you just let me go? Please! I'll tell you everything!"

I stare at the clippers and take in a breath. A single breath waiting for more information and then my gaze moves to Luke, my eyebrows raising in warning.

He looks to his left quickly, as if anything is there. He tries to get up as if the cuffs had disappeared. What he doesn't do, is give me the information I need.

The shirt is shoved back into his mouth and his ring finger goes next, leaving the middle finger on his left hand easily available for the next time I need to prove a point.

Tears leak from the man's eyes and his cries turn morbid as he mourns his mistake. I feel... I feel nothing but anger for him. Anger I don't show.

"Mr. Stevens, I read your file. You killed your mistress and then your wife. Or no," I feign a correction as I keep eye contact with Seth, not the man I'm determined to kill tonight. "Was it his wife first and then his mistress?"

"You've got it a little wrong, Boss," Seth tells me casually, the shirt still balled up in Luke's mouth, even though he's only crying, no longer screaming. "It was his sister and then his wife."

"No mistress then?"

Seth shakes his head in time with a sputtering of heaving coughs from Luke. "They stole his dope, or something like that." I stoop in front of the man and ask him, "Is that right?"

He's nodding his head even before the shirt's taken from him. As the damp cloth leaves his mouth, he nearly chokes trying to speak too soon. With a quick intake of air he explains himself. "They were going to take it all."

"Oh," I say and nod in understanding. "I see." Again I wipe the blades of the clippers on Luke's jeans. He glances down and then his head falls back as he tries desperately not to cry again.

"And you took Jenny Parks."

"I didn't take her!" He shakes his head as he denies what I said. And I wait a fraction of a second for him to explain. Which he does this time, the information flowing from his lips. "She wanted to go to Marcus. I was dropping her off! I was just supposed to drop her off at the bridge!"

"What bridge?"

"On Fifth and Park. The overpass." He nearly says more, but stops himself. With a knowing look I lean forward, but he continues. Just barely in time. "It's where I do all the drops for Marcus." His pale skin turns nearly white and his voice lowers. "Every three weeks or so, I have a pickup from out of state and a drop-off at the bridge. He gives an address. I go, pick up the unmarked package and drop it off at the bridge. A few weeks ago, he gave a name instead of an address. He told me to go to her, and to tell her Marcus was ready."

I can feel my brow pinch and a crease deepen in my forehead as I ask, "Do you know what he wanted with her?"

"No!" His head shakes violently with the answer. "I just had to pick her up and drop her off. That's all!"

"And what about the other drops?" I question him. "You ever take a peek at what's inside?"

Instead of answering, he swallows. Poor fucker.

His cry this time isn't at all like the last two. Seth covers his mouth as Luke's head falls back, and his middle finger drops to the grated floor alongside the other two severed extremities.

"Please, please." I know that's what he's saying behind the gag. *Please, stop.* I've heard it so many times in my life.

But in this world, there is no stopping.

I take a moment, wondering how he killed his wife. How he looked her in the eyes and stabbed her to death. Fourteen stab wounds. His sister was a gunshot to the back of the head. That one, that type of kill sounds like someone who stole from him. But fourteen stab wounds... that's anger. The twin sister of passion.

When Seth removes the shirt, Luke's head hangs heavy in front of him. He sucks in air like he's been going without it for too long. I could change that, but that's not in my favor.

"I want answers, Luke."

"Drugs. Lots of them. That's what the packages were."

"What kind of drugs?" I ask and for the first time, I grit my teeth, letting him hear the frustration.

He doesn't answer immediately and I stand up straighter, quickly gripping the hair at the back of his head and pulling it back so I can bring the clippers to his throat.

Seth takes a step back and I can feel his eyes on me, knowing this isn't the way it goes down. I couldn't give two shits about that right now.

"Heroin, coke, pot, you name it." Luke's answers are strained with his throat stretched out.

"And sweets?" I ask him.

The dumb fuck tries to nod and the blade slips across his skin. It's only a scratch, one he probably can't even feel with all the other pain rushing through him.

"Marcus doesn't need to deal. What's he doing with it?" I ask as I release him, turning my back to him and taking a few steps away to calm down.

"I don't know," is Luke's first answer but before I can even fully turn around the words rush out of him. "I think it's experiments and setups. He needs the drugs for planting them and I think a month or so ago, that deputy who OD'd? I think that was Marcus."

He insists he doesn't know after that, giving examples that he thinks Marcus may be responsible for, but not saying for sure that his guesses are true.

"You were in it for the money?" I question and to my surprise, the man shakes his head.

"At first... but then I wanted to be in with him. I wanted a place on his team."

The last sentence brings a chill to flow over my skin. "His team?"

Luke nods once. "I wanted to work with him."

"Marcus works alone," I tell him and he actually laughs. It's a sad, sick kind of laugh that graces his lips for only a fraction of a second, but then he shakes his head, looking me in the eyes. "That's not what Jenny said. She said he needed her. That she was going to make things right with Marcus."

"And what did you think that meant?" I ask him, feeling a frigid bite taking over my limbs. It grows colder and colder.

"That he was giving her an in to control it all."

"Control it all? You think that's what Marcus does?"

With hope fleeing Luke's eyes, he nods. "He has an army."

"And you think that's what Jenny was there for? To be in his army?" I ask him, getting closer to him.

He nods.

"Do you know anyone else in his army?"

He slowly shakes his head. "But she told me that's what

she was doing. She said she was joining his army."

An army of men working under Marcus. I share a look with Seth and he shrugs but doesn't look so sure.

"I'm not convinced," I say offhandedly and Luke's body jolts up as his voice raises. He's adamant it's the truth. All the while he continues to spill his thoughts that mean nothing to me, I consider what he's saying. There's simply no way Marcus would trust anyone to be involved with his plans.

"So what's he doing with Jenny then?" I raise my gaze to the now silent Luke Stevens. "What is he going to do with her?"

"I don't know. All I know is that I dropped her off securely. I held up my end of the bargain."

"And what did you get in return?" I ask him. He hesitates, but I don't bother removing anything else from him.

"Money," he finally answers. "Four grand."

"Is there anything else we should ask him?" I direct my question to Seth, who merely shakes his head before suffocating the man with his shirt.

Luke fights to breathe, but it's useless. It takes a few minutes and still Seth keeps the shirt over his face when Luke's body is motionless for another minute longer.

"You think he'll keep her alive?" I ask Seth once the rustling and muted screams have settled to silence.

"To start an army?"

I shake my head and agree with the expression on his face. That it's unrealistic for Marcus to have an army. It may have been what he led her to believe, but there is no army.

"Any reason at all that he'd keep her alive," I answer him.

"Marcus doesn't do loose ends." Seth's answer causes a chill to travel down the back of my neck. The feeling of loss and failure intertwine and wrap around my throat as I ask him, "What am I going to tell Bethany?"

His answer is simple and I already know it's what I should do, even if it's not what she'd want. "Nothing. Don't bring her into this any more than she already is."

CHAPTER 8

Bethany

T**HE COVERLESS BOOK PLAYS TRICKS ON ME.** I was certain Emmy's mother would fire the caretaker for poisoning her daughter. But she says it's only medicine that was poured into the soup. With the bottle in her hand, the mother does nothing but reprimand Emmy. She doesn't look any deeper into it. She only tells Jake that he's out of line and that Miss Caroline did nothing wrong. Emmy begs her mother to hire someone else and fire Miss Caroline, all to no avail.

Hate consumes me. For the women who are supposed to protect and love Emmy. And for the situation the young girl is in.

I read about how Jake is no longer welcome on the property, but Emmy sneaks out to see him, refusing to go on with life as she has been.

She doesn't eat what Caroline cooks so Caroline stops cooking for her altogether, crying outside of the kitchen all while Emmy cries in her bedroom and her mother does God knows what.

It's only at night that anything seems right. Only when Emmy climbs out of her bedroom window to meet Jake. It's the two of them against the world.

There's a passage that makes me feel alive, a passage that warms everything in my body.

"Take my hand and trust me," he tells her. "I promise to save you, because I love you."

That's what you do when you love someone, he said. You save them.

And that's where I had to stop.

Three more sentences are underlined. I don't have my journal with me though to add them to the list. It's useless to add them anyway. I've accepted that there's no message buried in the lines. Maybe Jenny just wanted me to read the story. Maybe she fell in love with Emmy and Jake like I have. So many maybes and questions that will never be answered.

I lay the book on its pages, so I don't lose where I'm at. I have to rub my eyes, and take a break after reading the last line I underlined, the line Emmy's mother told Jake. *Hope is a long way of saying goodbye.* It's in the book.

The words I gave to her, she saw it here. I wonder when she read it. Which came first. Not that it matters. None of it matters anymore.

I don't know why I bother to keep reading when it only makes me sad inside. When I know there's no message buried beneath the black and white letters.

A SINGLE KISS

It makes no sense at all, either, that I reach out to the phone to text Miranda, Jenny's friend who gave me the book.

I want to text Jenny and I'm conscious of that. I nearly do. I nearly text her, *Why this book? What did you want me to get from it?*

I'm not that crazy yet, so I text Miranda instead. Or maybe that makes me crazier. I'm not sure anymore.

Thank you for giving me the book.

It takes a minute before my phone vibrates in my hand with a response. *Bethany?*

Of course she wouldn't know it's me. Feeling foolish, I answer her, *Yes, I'm sorry to message, I just wanted to make sure I'd thanked you.*

You should know, when I saw her with that book and she was underlining it.... She said you would understand better then. She said you'd be happy.

I'd be happy?

Miranda is no one to me. I'd have been just fine never seeing her again... until my sister died. That changed so many things. She's a person I would never confide in, yet here I am, not hesitating to bleed out my every thought and emotion without recourse into a stream of texts. *I'm anything but happy. Maybe if she was truly invincible, I'd be better.*

Feeling the need to explain, I follow up my messages. *Sorry, it's a line in the book. She keeps saying she's invincible.*

I stare at her next message, reading it over and over. *So that's where she got it... she was saying that for a while before she packed.*

Packed? I think to myself. Why would she have packed?

Jenny didn't tell me that before.

I text her back, *Where did she go?*

Her answer is immediate. *I thought she went home to you. She didn't tell me where. I just assumed she was going back to you because she said she needed help.*

Jenny always said she wanted help, but she didn't really mean it. She only said it to get me off her back. It was always lies she told me.

But maybe that day, she was coming home. Maybe she finally wanted to get better. It's the sliding doors of life. If only one thing had changed, everything would be different. Maybe she was coming back home. Maybe that's when they got her. Maybe I was only minutes away from being back with her and they tore her from me.

I drop the phone onto the nightstand, not bothering to reply anymore.

Hating all the maybes, all the possibilities that could have, should have happened.

Everything stills for a moment, going out of focus. As if forcing me to embrace only one thing: She's gone. My sister is gone. My sister is gone, and I have nothing left. No one left but a man who I know is bad for me and one who will never love me.

The first tear that comes, I thought I could control. I can feel the telltale prickle, and how the back of my throat suddenly goes dry in that way that I know it's coming. I think I can keep it from slipping with a single long, deep breath. I think I can stop it and be just fine. I don't need a moment.

I thought so wrong. The first sob comes and in its wake and my failure to control it, heaving ugly sobs come bearing down on me. They're reckless, and unwarranted. Turning to my side, I bury my head in the pillow, wishing I could suffocate the sniveling wails that come from me without any consent at all.

I hate crying. I've always hated it.

The tears are hotter and larger as they slip down my heated face. Falling to my chin just below where my bottom lip quivers.

Jenny is gone. Such a simple thing, something I deal with constantly in work and have dealt with all my life. She's gone and there's nothing I can do about it.

The nightmares aren't real. She isn't hiding somewhere waiting for me to save her.

The book is only words; there's no deeper message within. It's only words, meaningless like Jase said they were.

It all means nothing.

I have nothing and I feel like nothing just the same. But why does nothing hurt so much? Why does it hurt this bad when you give up hope?

Something must find its way into hope's place in your heart. And that something feels like burning knives that keep stabbing me. I just want it all to stop. I want this chapter to end. Fuck, I need it to end. I can't live like this. I can't live in constant, all-consuming pain with nowhere to run.

Jenny, I hate you for leaving me. I hate you, but even hating you doesn't make the pain stop. I still love you and I don't think love can exist without hope.

It's funny how I cling to something that's not there. That I have faith that I'll see her again in another life. Or that if I somehow bring her justice, she'll know. That it will mean something to her, even if she's not here.

Settling back into the pillow, I lie there tired and feeling like I'm drowning. I start to think that it's okay to drown, that I shouldn't fight it anymore. I'm scared of what will happen when I stop fighting though. What happens when I sink lower and lower into the cold darkness?

That's the imagery that meets me in my sleep.

Jenny

It's almost been a month. Every day drags, achingly slowly. Every second wanting me to suffer more and more. It's worse than what I thought it would be. The nausea and shaking. I can't get over how cold I am all the time here.

There's nothing but cinder block walls and a mattress on the floor. If I could think for a moment, I'd remember where I am, but I don't remember. I can barely stand up without vomiting.

My bare knees scrape on the floor as I brace myself. The floor feels damp at first, like it's wet, but the palms of my hands are dry. Rocking my body back and forth, I try to just breathe through the aching pain, the sweating, the constant moving thoughts that only stay still when I see her. That's the only time everything settles, but it falls into the darkness where I hate myself for what I've done and what I've become.

The rumbling happens again, the gentle shaking of the light above my head. I'm not crazy. It's real. The room shakes every so often.

He told me I could sleep through it. Weeks of sleeping while my body goes through withdrawal. He said he'd take care of me, that I had a purpose in this world.

He said he'd help me. Marcus can't help me through this though. No one can help me. No one can save me from where my mind goes when I lie down.

I can't sleep anymore. Bethany's there every time I close my eyes and I feel sicker and full of guilt. I can't sleep through this, knowing what I did to her. What I sacrificed to be here.

"It'll all be worth it."

My eyes whip up to his when I hear his voice. "It hurts," is all I can say and I feel pathetic. Hurts isn't adequate. "I feel like I'm dying." The sentence is pulled from me, slowly, as it drags too. Everything drags so slowly.

"A part of you is dying." His voice holds no emotion, no remorse, no sympathy. It's only matter of fact. "And that's a good thing."

My head nods although I don't know that I agree. Some moments I do. Some moments I just want it to end. I know what would make it all stop; I know a needle would make it go away. I nearly beg for it, but the last time I did, he left me alone in here. "I thought it would only be weeks," I tell him, gripping on to that thread of a thought.

"It has only been weeks."

Shaking my head violently and then hating the spinning that comes after, I grip the sides of my head and rock again, trying to settle.

His voice carries softly to me, as if it's rocking me as well, "It's been close to a month. It's almost over. Just sleep."

"I don't want to sleep!" I scream at him, the words

clawing up my throat and scarring the tender flesh on their way out.

"Then don't." His answer is simple. In the dark corner of the room, he sits and watches. That's what he does. He observes. That's not what Beth would do. Licking the cracked skin on my bottom lip, I remember how she always had to be there, always involved, always telling me what I was doing wrong.

I wish I'd listened to her.

My rocking turns gentle just thinking about her.

"You said you'd tell her I was okay."

"I said I'll make sure she finds out." He corrects me sharply.

"Did she see it? The note Jeremy left for her?" His gaze meets mine when I say the name, we're not supposed to say each other's names. I know it's Jeremy though. He came in here to check on me the first few days. It had to be him because of the bandage on his chin.

Jeremy told me what Marcus did to his chin though. He said it was necessary and that's how I know it was him in the video Marcus showed me.

Jeremy's scar is not nearly as bad of a fate as what Luke would endure. Marcus said he deserved it. That it was meant to happen and to only tell him certain things. I listened; I was a good girl, but I regret it all right now. I want it all to stop. "Please," I whimper, "make it stop."

"It will stop in time and your sister will know in time." My sister. Bethany. I need her to know. "Things are going according to plan."

I comment, feeling hollow inside, "I just need her to know."

A SINGLE KISS

"Go to sleep, Jennifer." He knows the only person to call me Jennifer was my mother. I told him to stop, but all he says is that it's my name.

"I feel guilty," I confess to him as shivers run down my arms. I don't know why. Maybe because there is no judgment from him, only truth and facts no matter how cold and callous they are.

"You should," is his only answer.

"When will she know that I'm okay?" My eyes burn searching for him in the dark corner.

"That depends on something I can no longer predict."

"On what?" I ask him, feeling a new pain run down the seam of my chest.

"Jase Cross."

CHAPTER 9

Jase

SOME DAYS, BAD SHIT HAPPENS.
Some days you take a loss.
Other days, like today, the puzzle pieces to the overall bigger picture form and you can feel the bad shit and losses preparing to come. It's like watching it all tumble around you.

It's all I can think on the drive back home. That's it falling, everything is going to fall and I'm not sure how to stop it.

As I turn right onto the long gravel road, I feel the vibrations in the car and remember the footage played for Seth and me in the back room after we took care of Luke Stevens.

Declan finally got hold of video from a coffee shop's security feed of their parking lot that showed a section of the graveyard.

A young prick with a bandage covering half of his face snuck up on us and we had no fucking clue. He was right there, hiding behind the car and then at the windshield when the cop car came into view and I was focusing on that, rather than on him tucking a note in the wipers. He hid, crouched down by the wheel, but I should've seen his hand, I should have seen him walking up in the rearview by the tree line. I should have seen, but I didn't.

Marcus may truly be building an army; an army of faceless men like this prick. An army I don't have names for.

Seth's taking care of the surveillance at the bridge Luke mentioned. We have eyes everywhere, watching and waiting. But in order to see what's going on, something has to happen. Something has to fall. And I need names and faces to recognize.

The only one I have right now is Jenny Parks.

"Shit." The curse falls from my mouth as I pull up to my driveway to the estate, seeing the cop car in plain view. Officer Walsh is standing off to the right of the yard, looking out into the woods.

Just what I fucking need.

It's one thing after another. With the rise of adrenaline, my gaze instinctively goes to the second story window on the right, the curtains wide open, but Bethany nowhere to be found.

As I park the car and the faint music I wasn't listening to shuts off, a thought passes through me: *She wouldn't have called him.* There's no way he's here because of her.

With the car door opening, the bitter air hits me and it

only makes the sweat on my skin feel hotter.

"Officer Walsh," I call out, and my voice carries through the cold air. That's all I say to greet him, walking steadily past the cars to the yard where he stays put. He rocks on his heels as I slip my keys into my pocket. "Anything I can help you with?" I ask when I'm close enough to him.

"Beautiful view," he comments, taking his gaze back to the forest.

With the thin layer of snow and the white fog along the tree line, it's eerily beautiful.

I don't bother to comment, or to play with his niceties. If she called him, if she wanted to break me like that, get it over with. So I can deal with her and fix this shit.

She wouldn't do that, I think as I swallow, shoving both my hands in my pockets. The moment I glance at the trees, Officer Walsh finally looks back at me.

"I thought maybe if I told you something, you could tell me something," he says, and then clears his throat. A look crosses his face like he doesn't know if he's making the right move. Curiosity sneaks up on me and I give him a small nod as I say, "You first."

"My last case in New York... I failed to save a girl. She's all right now... but I didn't protect her like I should've. It's why I asked for reassignment. I failed her."

He doesn't look at me when he talks, so I take in every bit of his expression. Noting the sincerity in his voice. But wondering how good of a liar this prick is.

"She moved back here. Close to here, anyway."

"That why you're here?" I ask him. "Are you looking for her?"

"No, not looking," he answers me but still doesn't look

at me. "I know where she is."

A breeze rushes by, causing his coat to slip open for a moment. His badge shows, just as the gun in his holster is on display for the moment. He shifts and buttons up his coat as he talks.

"I'm looking for someone else. A man named Marcus. He's the one who *saved* her." He rolls his shoulder back as he says "saved" and a grimace mars his face. "He's the one who got her out of that mess." His gaze finally meets mine when he adds, "He got her into it though. He used her, and then claims to have saved her."

His jaw clenches and an anger I haven't seen from him is left unchecked. It's evident in the way his shoulders tense, plus the way he breathes out heavily. And in his voice when he says, "Marcus put her through a hell that I can't even imagine surviving."

Emotion drenches his confession and I can feel the vendetta that wages war in his eyes.

"What is it you want from me?"

"I want Marcus." His answer is immediate. "Anything you have on him."

I swallow, hesitating and Officer Walsh shakes his head with disgust. "You know him. I know you do. I've read the files and all the paperwork. For a decade or more, you and your brothers' names have been right there along with his."

"Sure," I tell him, "Names on paperwork. But Marcus doesn't have a face, he doesn't have a number to call, he doesn't have a location. There's not a damn thing I can give you on Marcus." I'm surprised by the resentment that laces itself around every sentence that's spoken.

"If I could hand over Marcus to you, I would. Because

I don't know what he's thinking or why he does the shit he does," I say with finality, and then question my own statement.

Officer Walsh considers me for a long moment, maybe waiting for more.

"I don't have anything for you, Officer."

"If you're not with me, you're against me," he responds lowly. "You know that?"

"Words to live by," I comment with a nod and this time I'm the one staring off into the woods.

"If you do find something, would you even consider telling me?" he asks and I can feel his eyes burning into me.

"I wish you all the luck in the world," I tell him and then breathe in deep, debating on answering his question truthfully, lying or simply not answering at all. I settle for the last option and ask him, "Is there anything else I can help you with?"

"What's that?" That's the first thing Bethany says to me as I set the large cardboard box down in the middle of the bedroom. She didn't respond when I walked in; she remained under the covers, in the same position she was in when I left.

Her brunette hair tumbles down her body as she raises herself off the bed. Off my bed. That knowledge does something to me, as does the white light from the open curtains kissing her skin.

"Did I wake you?" I ask her rather than answering her

question. The look of sleep plays on her face, making me eager to get in bed with her. As she sits up, crossing her legs in bed and pulling the covers into her lap, her baggy sleepshirt falls off her shoulder and she has to readjust it.

"Only for a minute I think. It's been hard getting to sleep," she answers as I climb into bed, and it groans with her words.

"Just a single minute?" I tease her, wanting to put a smile on her face. She gives me a small one, accompanied with the roll of her eyes. It's my cue to lean forward, taking a single kiss from her. She's still guarded, still giving me questioning gazes and still stiff when I reach out and place my hand on her thigh.

Tucking her hands into her lap she doesn't answer me, she only shrugs and then those hazel eyes look up at me, peeking through her thick lashes.

"I went to your place," I say to change the subject, getting off the bed to go to the box and needing to get away from the look in her eyes.

I grab the pills out of the box. They're years old; we don't even make sweets in the pill form anymore. But I would never throw this bottle away. "I thought you may want some more of your things. Grabbed some mugs, your throw blanket, stuff like that."

She says thank you softly and then clears her throat to say it again louder.

"You brought my mugs?" she questions me with her brow furrowed and it only makes her look cuter. Her legs are bare as she makes her way to the box, the t-shirt stopping just past her ass.

"You have a lot of them on the counter with that box

of tea." I shrug as I sit on the bed, watching her go through the box and staring at her ass as she does. "Thought you'd like them."

She takes a few things out of the box, setting them on my dresser behind her and lining up her computer, charger and a few other things in a row.

"Why are you like this?"

Her question catches me off guard. "Like what?"

"Why are you trying to make me happy... I don't understand what you want from me."

I would be frustrated if she wasn't genuinely curious. "Did you expect me to keep you here with nothing of your own?"

"I don't know what to expect," she says, and the honesty in her voice is raw and transparent.

"Right now, I want you to stop fighting me."

She smiles wide for the first time since I've walked in, staring down at an owl mug in her hand. It's a sad, soft smile. "Fighting is what I do best though. Came into the world fighting, I'll leave it that way."

I can't help but return the smile to her. "That's fine with me, cailín tine. Just don't fight with me."

"You okay?" she asks me, setting down the mug and stalking over to me. I lean forward and pull her petite body between my legs, resting my hands on the small of her back before I answer her.

"I had a long day."

I lower my head to rest in the crook of her neck and she does the same. Her lips leave a small kiss that rouses desire from me.

Just as I'm ready to take her, to lay her on the bed and

fuck away my problems, she stops me, pulling away to tell me, "I did nothing today."

"Some days that's good to do, to just heal and let the world move around you."

"That's one way to put it."

Every ounce of lust dampens, seeing her lack of life. Fire dies when it's closed off and not allowed to breathe.

I want her to breathe, but she's suffocating herself.

"Did you go to the kitchenette?" I ask her and she shakes her head.

"I didn't leave the bedroom."

"I need to show you around," I comment, noting that she's been like this for a few days. Listless. Depressed. "You can't just lie around and expect to get better."

"Get better?" she bites back, her eyes flashing with indignation. "There is no 'getting better,' Mr. Cross. I'm simply trying to adapt to my new reality and I don't have a damn thing to distract me."

She stands up straighter, squaring her shoulders and leaning closer to me. "I may be taking up residence in your bed. I may do all sorts of shit with you I'd never tell a soul I craved so badly, but you," she points her finger to my chest and then licks her lower lip. The act distracts me and instantly I want to take her, punish her for tempting me. "You can tell me how you want me in bed. You can boss me around while I crawl on all fours for you, I don't give a fuck." She shrugs halfheartedly and her shirt slips off her shoulder. She knows what she's doing to me. The little smirk on her lips dims though when she looks me in the eyes and tells me, "You don't get to tell me how to live my life."

"I wasn't," I respond and I'm surprised by the sudden change. The hot and cold between us.

"I want you, I'm not afraid to admit that. Even now, when I'm not able to do what I love, I can't go into work. I'm afraid to go back to my own home," she admits and swallows, looking anywhere but at me and crosses her arms. "And I'm coming to terms with the fact that everyone in my family has died tragically and there wasn't a damn thing I could do about it." She shakes her head.

"Even now, I want you and I love the distraction of you." Her fingers linger on my chest and she steals a quick kiss before whispering down my neck as she pulls herself away from me. "But you don't get to tell me what to do or how to mourn. You'd be wise to remember that, Jase."

That's my cailín tine. Not hidden deep down, just failing to find a reason to come out. I'll give her a reason. I can give her that.

"Tell me something," she says and takes a seat on the black velvet chair next to the dresser. She lays her head back against the wall and pulls her legs into her chest.

"What do you want to know?"

"Who is Angie? What happened to her?"

Surprise lights inside of me, along with dread. "Why are you asking?"

"One time you said I reminded you of someone. Do I remind you of her?"

"She's not the one you remind me of." As I answer her, every muscle in my body tightens.

"Is that where you learned to do those things? The fire? With Angie?"

"No," I answer her again, feeling my throat go dry.

"Well then who the hell is she?" she questions flatly, shaking her head.

"She's someone who died a while back."

"I'm sorry," she whispers and I tell her it's okay although the tension grows between us.

"Do you want to talk about it?" she asks and I shake my head no.

"Everyone dies, Jase, that doesn't define her as to who she was." I don't think Bethany's aware of the magnitude that her words have. "Who was she?"

"A girl who died because of my mistakes."

"And I don't remind you of her?" she questions again, a dullness taking over her gaze.

"No."

As she goes through the things I brought her, I go to the bathroom, placing the pills where they belong. In the same spot Angie left them. The pills were hers and they've been there since the day she died. Not this same medicine cabinet, but the same location. Bottom shelf on the right. That's where she put them.

The irony isn't lost on me that Bethany took them. I stare back at myself in the mirror after I close the medicine cabinet and wonder if I should've left Beth alone. If I never should have tainted her by knocking on her door almost two weeks ago.

"Well," she says, sitting up straighter and making her way to the bed behind me. "Since it's already uncomfortable I might as well tell you, I did some math."

"Go on," I tell her when she breathes in deep, pulling the comforter all the way up. I suppose she got cold.

"One hundred dollars every ten minutes. That's

fourteen thousand, four hundred every day. Which would mean the debt is paid in twenty-one days. Not months."

The semblance of a grunt leaves me and I run my thumb along my bottom lip. The only sweet distraction from this conversation is that her eyes lower, lingering on my lips and her own lips part.

"So if you're wanting me to stay here," she starts, staring at my lips as she speaks. Standing up, I walk as she talks, so I can stand across from her. "I want it in writing that the debt won't exist after twenty more days."

Leaning against the dresser, I cross my arms and gaze down at her. "You think you earned fourteen thousand dollars yesterday?"

Indignation flashes in her eyes. "The deal was time, nothing else. And I gave you all my time and listened to you." Her throat tightens as she swallows and my gaze falls to her collarbone and then lower.

"You stay with me for twenty days, which I'm doing to protect you-"

"Which I didn't ask for." She's quick to cut me off. "In fact, I think we can both agree I was resistant but did it because it's what you wanted."

"No good deed goes unpunished, huh?"

"It was never my debt," she rebuts.

Time passes with each of us staring at the other, waiting for the other one to give.

"You listen to everything I say for forty days—"

Again she cuts me off. "Twenty."

"No fucking way," I answer her, keeping my voice low. "Sleep doesn't count as listening to me."

"Thirty max, including yesterday, so twenty-nine

days." Her voice is strong as she negotiates. I have to focus not to glance down at her breasts and the way they peek up from her crossed arms.

"Twenty-nine days of you doing whatever it is that I want?" I ask her, feeling my cock go rigid. I unzip my pants and let them drop to the floor so she can see.

Color rises from her chest to her cheeks. She swallows, watching me stroke myself as she answers. "Twenty-nine days," she agrees.

"Get over here and get on your knees." I barely get the words out before she's moving, kicking the sheets away so they don't trip her up.

She takes me into her mouth and I shove my cock in deeper, gripping her hair so I can control it.

Before she can choke, I pull her back and listen to her heave in a breath. She stares up at me with eagerness, her hands grabbing the back of my thighs.

"I'm going to use you and get my money's worth, cailín tine."

❦

Sleep's dragging her under. I can admit I'm exhausted as well. Not in the same way, but I can't go to sleep. I don't want tonight to end.

"I can still feel you," she whimpers. The sheets rustle between her legs as she moans softly, pushing her head into the pillow and letting the pleasure ring in her blood.

Her eyes are half lidded as she peeks up at me. "Does it feel the same for you?" she asks.

I let the tip of my nose play along her cheek and then

nip her earlobe. "Does it feel drawn out to you? Like wave after wave and a single touch would make the next crash on the shore?"

Her eyes close as she breathes in deep and steady.

"Sex certainly changes things, doesn't it?" I ask her, remembering how only hours ago I worried about where her mind was headed. She hums in agreement.

I pull the sheet down from her chest slowly, exposing her all the way down to her waist. A shudder rolls through her and with a single tug on her nipples, they harden for me.

"Jase," she murmurs my name.

"I'm not done with you yet," I tell her and her hazel eyes widen.

"I stored the lighter and alcohol pads in the nightstand yesterday, hoping to play with you this morning, but you were asleep."

She huffs a small playful laugh as I open the drawer, still lying in bed. "Is that why you said sleeping doesn't count?"

Keeping one small pad folded, I run it along her closest breast and then pluck the other one, letting the moisture cool on her skin and sparking her nerve endings.

Sweet sounds of rapture slip through her lips as her hands make their way between her legs. She doesn't touch herself though, not until I tell her, "It's all right to play with yourself, but be still."

The fire blanket is in the drawer, I remind myself of that as I flick the lighter, staring at the flame and then gently bringing it to where the ethanol is still lingering on her skin. The flame grows along her skin, licking and turning a brighter yellow, but it's gone just as quickly as it came. By the time her mouth has parted, the evidence of it is all gone.

"Again," I tell her, sucking the other nipple into my mouth and running my teeth along her tender flesh before moving back to her right side, wiping the alcohol pad around her areola and then lighting it aflame again.

This time she moans louder, her knees pulling up the sheet that's puddled around her waist.

"Do you know why I enjoy fire?" I ask her, massaging and pinching her left breast once again.

"Because it's dangerous," she answers me softly and I shake my head no.

"Because it's wild," I correct her and then do it again, a larger portion this time.

Once the fire's gone, I grip both her breasts in my hands and run my thumbs over both nipples.

"Which one makes you feel more alive, cailín tine?"

CHAPTER 10

Bethany

I SUPPOSE I WAS NEVER UNDER THE ILLUSION THAT it was a tit for tat of information. So long as he answers my questions and keeps searching for answers I'll never be able to find, I'll willingly warm his bed.

In fact, I have little to no objection to it at all.

It's obvious I'm a fool, that I have no grip on reality, let alone my own mind. I feel like I'm losing it to be honest. What's the point in trying to stay afloat in the middle of the deep dark ocean when there's no land in sight? I could fight it, and I feel like I have, like I'm exhausted from fighting to stay above water. Or I can fall into Jase's arms, and let him hold me for a moment.

Fear plays a small part, but it's shocking how small a part it is.

Someone is after me, and this arrangement prevents

them from getting whatever it is they want from me—which can't be good—and could lead me to information. Although that piece... that last piece about information. I'm starting to lose hope for that to happen.

I'm starting to accept it never happening.

If I think about it like I'm an undercover cop, suddenly it's all okay in my mind.

That's what I tell myself anyway. It's all pretend. My life is turning into a tall tale like Marky used to feed me. And that makes the jagged pill easier to swallow.

These are the thoughts that lead me to biting my thumbnail as I lie in Jase's bed. The clock on his nightstand, a beautiful contemporary clock with a minimalistic face of sleek marble and only hands to tell the time, must be lying to me because it reads that it's after noon already.

I sink back under the covers, pulling them up easily since I'm in bed alone and listen to the ticking. My hand splays under the sheets onto the side of the mattress where Jase lay last night. The thought of last night brings a faint kiss of a smile to my lips, but it falls just as quickly as it came, finding the bedsheet cold to the touch.

I called work again when I first woke up, ready to leave a message this time. Half of me wanted to be professional and ask what the phone call regarded, the other half wanted to call my boss an asshole, assuming it was him. Instead of leaving a message, I found myself talking to the lead nurse on Michelle's case.

"I'm so sorry," she started and then immediately dove into discussing the restraints they had to use on her arms. "She was eating the gauze, Beth. I have no idea what to do with her other than restrain her. I've never had a patient with pica and I don't know what to do."

"She loves pickles. So make pickle ice." I rattled off what I'd been doing with Michelle. She's a new patient, pregnant and newly diagnosed with pica. It's a psychological disorder where patients have an appetite for non-nutritive foods, or even harmful objects. "It'll most likely diminish after the pregnancy."

"I know, but what am I supposed to do?" The stress and frustration were all too relatable. "She can't stay restrained for six months."

"Listen to me," I said as I gripped the phone tighter. "Mix half pickle juice and half water, add in a soluble supplement, freeze into ice chips and then give them to her throughout the day, constantly."

"That can't be it."

"I'm telling you, you keep that by her bedside and she eats it slowly. Something about the cold makes her pace herself."

"Okay... okay," Marilyn sounded hopeful and I felt it too, until I heard someone ask who she was talking to and then the line went dead. When I get back to work, I'm going to kill my boss. I can hear his excuse now, that I'm a workaholic and I wouldn't be able to help myself, but that they should know better.

That was the only distraction I had.

I'm slow to sit up, forcing myself to rise although I have no plans, no control, nothing at all I want to do... but read I suppose. Thank all that's holy for books.

The small piece of me that anticipated—and looked forward to a note from Jase—is disappointed when I find his nightstand empty of any slip of paper.

I shouldn't feel so hollow in my chest. I shouldn't feel this kind of loss.

Bringing my knees up to my chest, I rest my cheek on my right knee and wonder what happened to me. What the fuck happened to the woman I was? Without work... I'm no one. My life is utterly empty and the one thing that's filling it shouldn't be in my life at all.

One breath, and the screaming thoughts quiet. Two breaths and I find it hard to care. This will all be over soon. It's temporary and nothing more. I'll be back to work, unraveled or not.

Until then... I'll read and let Jase fuck me. Maybe one day, I'll even get out of bed.

The Coverless Book
Three quarters through the book

Emmy

I remember all the times Miss Caroline took me to the appointments. Mother always met me there. It was Miss Caroline who took me on long drives and told me stories the whole way. No matter how many hours it was. That's all I can remember as we sit outside of the shed. It's a large shed, with running water and an outhouse with plumbing around the back.

Jake said it's his cousin's place, so it's okay that we stay here.

I can remember the trips to the hospitals. The long drives we took to get to them. The hotels we stayed in. Miss Caroline always stopped for ice cream on the way to and back. And she let me eat all sorts of things I never had at home.

I remember all those trips... but those are the only trips I've ever taken.

Until this one.

"What's wrong?" Jake's voice breaks my thoughts. His hand cradles my chin. "You look like you regret this." I hate how his voice sounds like he really believes that.

My hair tickles my shoulders when I shake my head and tell him, "You're crazy to think that. I love you, Jake." He needs to know that. "I was just hoping to go inside. It's been a few days since we've slept on a bed." I want to give myself to him. But not like this.

His lips part and instead of words coming out, he closes them again, kicking the rubble under his shoes. "We can't go inside, Em." He stares off at the large farmhouse. "Your mom filed a report and the sheriff called. We can't go inside."

Feeling a wave of nausea, I lower my head to my hands. "Your family doesn't know we're here?"

"My cousin does, and he's bringing us blankets. I've got money once we get out of this town. But, for tonight... Our parents are looking for us."

The crickets from the cornfield get louder as the sun sets deeper behind the crimson sky. It's nearly dusk already.

"I'm sorry I can't give you more right now, but soon I can."

I find his hand in mine, and tell him, "It's why running away is so scary. The unknown."

His eyes stare deep into mine as he says, "The only known in my life I need, is you beside me. As long as I have you, nothing else matters."

He tells me he loves me and I feel that drop in my stomach again, but I make sure I tell him I love him too and that

I can't wait for all of the unknowns I'll face with him.

That's just before I go around the back of the shed to where the faucet is to wash my face. It's just before I get sick in the field. It's just before I look down at my hands as I'm cleaning myself up and see nothing but blood.

Three more times, I cough up blood and my eyes water. My face heats and then all at once, it stops. It's not a lot, it's not a lot of blood. It's because of whatever Miss Caroline put in the soup for all that time. I know it is. She made me sick. I'll get better now; Jake knows that too. I'm not sick, I'm recovering from what she did to me.

I hide what happened from Jake, though, all the blood I just coughed up. I don't want him to see.

I just want to be loved and to love him. Isn't love enough?

"Are you okay?"

Hearing Jase before I see him startles me. I hadn't noticed how erratic my breathing was until he came in. I set the book down on the nightstand.

"Yeah, why?" I ask him as I rub my eyes, and try to come back to reality. I catch a glimpse of the clock and realize nearly two hours slipped by. The uneasiness and shock that the book left me in won't shake off when I look back up to Jase.

"You look horrified."

I answer him, "It's just a book."

"What happened?" he asks me like he really cares as he takes off a black cotton shirt, damp with sweat. His body glistens, his muscles flex with every movement and with the increase of lust, the problems of my fictional world fall away.

"She might really be sick," I tell him, although my eyes stay glued to his chest.

"Who?" He stands still, a new shirt in his hand as he waits for my answer.

"Don't worry about it," I tell him. "She's invincible." Hearing those words come from me with confidence makes my stomach drop.

Jase has a different reaction. His lips pull up into an asymmetric smile at my remark and the way his eyes shine with humor is infectious. I feel lighter, but still, the sickness of the unknown churns in my stomach.

"I can't stay here," I tell him, knowing I need to do something and just as aware that there's nothing for me to do here. He removes the space between us, climbing up onto the bed to sit cross-legged in front of me. He doesn't love me like… like I feel for him. That's the truth that sinks me further into the bed.

Being around him, knowing what I feel for him and coming to terms with that, but not feeling the same from him… it's killing me. It makes me want to run. It's scary when you realize you love someone and that they may never feel the same for you. Not in the same way. Nothing like what I feel for him.

It doesn't stop me from breathing him in though.

The sweet smell of his sweat is surprising… and heady. The way he looks at me, it's all the more intoxicating.

"You agreed to twenty-nine days," he reminds me.

"Twenty-eight now," I correct him in return.

"Twenty-eight then."

"I can't stay here like this. Doing nothing day in, day out."

"I don't expect you to."

"What am I supposed to do?" I ask him, truly needing an answer.

He considers me for a moment. "I really don't know what to do," I tell him when he hesitates to answer me. It's harder for me to admit that than I thought it would be.

"I don't have any answers for you," he tells me beneath his breath, quietly, like he's sorry.

"I love work. I want to go back to work."

"I don't know that you're in the right mindset to do that."

My voice rises as I ask, "How am I supposed to get better when I have nothing to do to make me better?"

"Time." He answers me with a single word, joining me on the bed. "You could start with putting your mugs in the kitchen." Looking at the box still where he left it yesterday, he tells me, "You could do whatever you like."

"I can't leave," I answer him boldly, letting him know it pisses me off.

"Yesterday I didn't want you to, no. But that doesn't mean you can't leave. I'm not trapping you here, you're locking yourself in this room."

I hate him for his answer, although I don't know why.

"Where would you go after you're done with work to let loose?" he asks me.

"A bar."

"I like that," he says and scoots closer to me, pulling me into his lap. I settle against him, resting my back to his front.

"You order wine or mixed drinks at the bar?"

"Mixed. Vodka and whatever the bartender wants."

The rough chuckle makes his chest shake gently and I love the feeling of it. His stubble brushes my neck as he asks, "And then?"

"Grocery store if I need to, although I really only keep K-cups and cardboard pizza in the fridge."

"Cardboard pizza?"

"You know, the kind that come in a box and you put in the toaster oven?"

That makes him laugh too. The sound of him laughing eases everything.

"You have a pretty smile," he tells me and his voice is calming.

"You have a pretty smile too," I tell him back and he makes a face.

He changes the subject quicker than I expect. "We don't know who broke in."

My own smile falters and I stare at my fingers, picking absently under my nails at nothing.

"I know that's not what you wanted to hear and it's not what I was hoping to tell you. But there are no fingerprints, no cameras anywhere."

With his hand on my chin, he forces me to look at him as he explains, "We looked into everyone's surveillance cameras, Beth. It's not quite legal, but they'll never know. Whoever it was left no trace at all."

"So I'll never know and they could come back." I'm surprised how much pain accompanies that knowledge. My chest feels like it's been hollowed out and bricks put in the place of whatever it is I need to survive.

"No. That's not true. We have a lead on your sister," he tells me with hope and authority.

"A man named Luke Stevens. He's no one around here, but he was seen with your sister before she went missing."

He hands me a picture of a man I've never laid eyes on. He's got to be in his forties, with a clean-cut look to him and I could only imagine what the hell Jenny would have been doing with someone like this.

"You think he did it?" I dare to ask Jase.

"I'm not sure, but I'm going to find him and get as much information as I can from him, cailín tine."

"Miranda told me she packed her bags," I say and swallow thickly, needing to calm the adrenaline racing in my blood. "She said Jenny packed before she went missing." The image of my sister doing just that and then leaving with this man plays in my mind. "Maybe she was in love with him," I surmise.

"I don't think—" Jase bites down to stop himself from saying something else.

"What?"

His inhale is uneven and he looks past me before saying, "I just wanted you to know that I'm working on it. But don't do this. Don't let your mind play tricks on you. All we know is that he was seen with her."

"Seen doing what?"

"Getting into a truck around the time she went missing but they aren't positive of the date."

I have no words as the theory in my mind unravels.

"It could be nothing, but we have a name and I'm working on it," he tells me and takes my hand in his, stopping me from my mindless habit.

"So now there are two names?" I ask, remembering the last time we talked about information.

He nods once, but doesn't give me the other name. The one he promised wouldn't help me.

"Which do you think broke into my house?" I ask him and instead of answering, he tells me, "I'm having Seth install a top-of-the-line security system. Everything will be repaired, and all the locks will be changed."

The information sparks a reaction I don't expect and I have to pull my hand away, but he doesn't let me so I blurt out the question, "You want me to go back... to my place?"

"No," he says and his quick answer alleviates some of the unwanted stress. "I'd prefer you here by my side and for the next twenty-eight days, I want you here at my place. But you need to be able to go home and feel safe. I get that and I wanted to make sure it was safe."

I can only nod, feeling overwhelmed and not knowing what to do. When he squeezes my hand, I squeeze back and tell him, "Thank you."

"I have to go. Late-night meeting."

Late meeting. My lips stay closed although I don't have to say anything at all. My gaze drops just as my lightheartedness does. I can never forget the life Jase leads. I need to remember.

"Don't look at me like that." His voice is low and a threat lays behind the words.

"Like what?" I ask him as if I don't know what he's referring to.

"Like I'm less than you for what I do."

"I don't," I protest, hating that it's obvious.

"You do."

Biting back my pride, I apologize, "I'm sorry."

"It's never going to change, Bethany. This isn't something I can run away from."

He stares at me like he's repentant. Like he'd change it if he could, although I don't believe him. All I can tell him back is, "I didn't ask you to."

CHAPTER 11

Jase

I'M THE LAST TO ENTER THE KITCHEN AND AS I make my way to the counter, Carter pushes a tumbler with ice and whiskey my way.

"You want to meet her, huh?" I ask Carter, looking him in his eyes as I bring the glass to my lips and let the liquor settle on my tongue to burn.

Carter only lets a smirk show, filling the empty tumbler in front of him and then asking Declan if he wants a glass too.

"I'll have beer," Declan announces and Daniel looks over his shoulder at Declan, a grin on his face too before reaching into the fridge. The bottles clink together and the telltale sound of the beer fizzing fills up the silence as I wait for my answer.

"You told her not to come in here, didn't you?" he asks,

the smile only widening.

"You're a prick," I tell my oldest brother and when they all chuckle, I finally let myself smile and pull out the barstool. I'm a prick for lying to her too, but they don't need to know that.

"If she met us, if she knew what was going on, maybe she'd feel a little differently," Sebastian says as he enters the room, touching his elbow to Carter's in greeting and taking the last tumbler of whiskey.

"Maybe," I agree although I'm quick to take another swig of the whiskey.

"What's the update on Addison?" Sebastian asks Daniel. His response is to share a look with Carter first. They're going through the next stage of life together. All three of the men although Sebastian's wife is furthest along. Daniel and Carter just found out about the pregnancies.

Daniel picks at the label on his beer bottle as he answers, "They said it's just high blood pressure. She just needs to take it easy."

A moment passes where no one knows what to say. Addison never thought she could get pregnant and for good reason. She went through a rough life as a child.

"Aria's happy that she gets to pick out everything with a friend," Carter says to break up the tension.

Sebastian contributes to the easy feeling by remarking, "Chloe's happy she won't be the only fat one." He adds quickly, "Or so she said," which gets a good laugh and a clink of beers and glass tumblers.

"It feels good having all five of us in here, doesn't it? Like old times," Declan comments.

All four of my brothers and the one man, Sebastian, who sticks out because he's older.

"We do have a real reason to meet," Carter says and glances at the closed door behind me. She can place her hand to the panel and enter, or simply try to listen from the other side of the door.

"Romano." Daniel and I say our enemy's name at once.

Carter nods. "He's scattered. There's no doubt."

"What made him run?" Sebastian asks.

"He's outnumbered. It's not just Talvery men looking to settle a vendetta, but us too. It's quiet with Officer Walsh and the FBI leaning hard on the local cops," Daniel answers and Carter nods along with him. "If he was ever going to leave, now is the time to do so."

"If he comes back, which he has to in order to get everything out of his warehouses, all of his supply and the stashed guns are on Fourth. If he comes back, there are only two roads he can use to come into town," I comment, knowing if he comes back, I don't want to give him another chance to leave.

"You think he'll come back for it?" Sebastian asks.

"He's got money hidden away in the warehouse on Fourth, we've staked out that street and he knows, but he doesn't know that we're aware his money's there. Maybe he thinks with him gone, we'll forget about him," Carter answers him.

"Forget about him?" There's a tension in Daniel's voice, akin to outrage. "We aren't going to let him run."

Daniel's comment goes unanswered.

"I say we blow up his estate and the warehouse too. Destroy everything."

"He left men behind." Carter's quick to rebut my suggestion.

"Not enough," I answer him, staring into his eyes.

"With the FBI and former agent on our asses, do we really want to risk it?" Declan asks, wanting to be safe.

"Yes. We do. We can't let what he did go unanswered. We can't let anyone think they can run from us," Daniel says, his body tense and the beer he has in his hand tapping against the granite.

"Calm down," Carter tells our brother, but I'm with Daniel.

"He's right," I say to voice my opinion.

"Destroy everything in his name and send Nikolai after him," Daniel suggests.

"Nikolai?" A tension coils in my stomach. "He tried to kill me; he tried to take Addison, your soon-to-be wife." I can't help that my voice rises, the same outrage Daniel had a moment ago slipping into my cadence.

"Do you plan to chase him, Jase? You going to risk your... what's her name? Bethany? Are you going to risk her to chase after him?" he questions me.

"Sending Nikolai is smart," Declan adds and Sebastian nods in agreement. I crack my neck, not looking at my brothers, knowing they're not on my side. All while questioning if they're right. If I could really risk leaving Bethany behind.

"With Marcus still here... you're right. We should send Nikolai."

"Aria will never forgive me if something happens," Carter admits and stares into the swirling whiskey in his glass.

"She doesn't have to know," Declan says which brings all of our eyes to him.

"It's easy to say that, but they always find out. The truth always rises to the surface." Sebastian's sentiment sends a chill down my spine. I warm it with the remainder of the whiskey in my glass.

The empty tumbler hits the granite in time with the door opening behind us. All five of us turn to see Bethany, standing in the now open doorway with her hand still in the air.

The sight of her is enough to ease the tension in the room.

"You look like a deer in headlights," Daniel comments and then waves her in.

"I'm sorry," she says immediately, not moving an inch. "I didn't mean to interrupt."

"Were you planning on just sneaking around then?" Carter asks and grins at her. "We can pretend we didn't see you if that's the case." The ice in his tumbler clinks as he brings it up to his smile and takes a sip.

The long sweater hangs loosely on her, but when she wraps her arms around herself, I can just barely make out the dip in her waist. With keys jingling in her hand, and seeing as how she's slipped on leggings and boots, it's obvious she's heading out.

Doubt sinks its claws into me. Holding me in place as she stands there. Bethany's wide eyes meet mine and she nearly turns around when I don't say anything.

"Come meet my brothers," I say loud enough to stop her in her tracks before she can run off completely.

She hesitates a moment and then walks to my side, her

insecurity showing. The moment she's beside me, I wrap my arm around her waist.

"I'm sorry," she whispers although it's not low enough that the rest of the guys wouldn't hear.

"Guys, meet Bethany. Sebastian, Carter, Daniel and Declan." I point at each of them one by one and she gives them a small, embarrassed wave. "Sebastian's not blood, but still family," Carter comments and then fills his glass and mine again. "Want a drink?" he offers her.

"That's actually why I came in here," she says and Daniel interrupts her by saying, "I like her already," which gets agreeable laughter from the rest of the guys.

Her nerves are still high, no matter how much I run soothing circles along her back. Her voice is strained when she looks up at me and says, "I forgot I told a friend I was seeing her tonight. It's the weekend. I was just going to head out."

It's more than obvious to not just me, but to all of the men standing here that she's searching for permission.

It's not like her, I wish they could see her. Really see her. I tell myself she just needs time.

"Have fun." With that I smile down on her, not giving her any restraints. Seth and his men will watch her and inform me.

Blinking, she holds back the obvious questions that beg to be spoken. Instead she only nods and nearly says thank you, but those words turn into an, "Okay, I'll see you tonight?"

My brothers and Sebastian say nothing, only observing and drinking. I know they're judging, and I hate them for it.

I can see her need to run and before she can turn and leave me, I capture her lips with mine. Her lips are hard at first, and she utters a small protest of shock, right before she melts into me. Her lips soften and her hands move to my back when I deepen the kiss just slightly.

It doesn't last long, but it lasts long enough to bring color to her cheeks. With her teeth sinking into her bottom lip, she smiles sweetly and barely glances at my brothers, giving them a wave before quickly walking away.

I leave the door open, watching her walk out of sight.

"She seemed nervous."

"No shit," Carter says and laughs off Declan's comment at the same time Sebastian asks for another beer.

"What are you doing with her?" Carter asks me and everyone goes quiet. "It seems different from what you mentioned." All eyes are on me as I stand alone.

I can feel all of their eyes on me, the questions piling on one after the other in their gazes. With my forearms on the cold, hard counter, my shoulders tense. I lower my gaze to my folded hands firmly placed on the granite.

"That's a damn good question."

CHAPTER 12

Bethany

It feels like there was a heavy bell that rang too close to me. That's the only way I can describe how I'm feeling. The sound left a ringing sensation on my skin, maybe even deeper.

Every minute on my drive home I thought it would go away, but it didn't.

It tingles, and refuses to go unnoticed. Even now as I sit with Laura in the parking lot outside of a strip mall with a bottle of cabernet half gone and tempting me to take another swig… the ringing doesn't stop. I'm trapped in the moment when it happened. When the world shifted and made it impossible for me to get away from the giant bell.

The moment Jase kissed me like a lover in front of his brothers.

I've heard of Sebastian Black; my sister went to school with him. I've heard of the Cross Brothers. I've seen Carter from afar at The Red Room once. To be in a room with such men, with intimidating, dangerous men, I couldn't think or breathe. It was a mix of fear and something else. Something sinful.

Even with them talking, joking, acting as if it was just an ordinary day and ordinary people in an ordinary kitchen, I couldn't shake all the stories I'd heard of these men.

But then Jase kissed me.

Every part of my body has woken up, and it refuses to let the memory become that, a memory. It's holding on to it instead, trying to stay there. Going out with Laura has definitely dampened the ringing, but not so much though that I can't feel it still, even hours later.

"What's wrong with you? You love this song." Laura cuts through my hazy thoughts and my gaze moves from the yellow streetlights and lit signs of the chain stores to focus on her instead.

I hadn't even noticed music was playing.

"Hey," Laura says and pats my arm as she leans forward with a hint of something devious in her voice. "You know how..." she shifts uneasily and restarts. "You remember how you helped me interview for the position at the center?"

"Of course," I answer her and wonder where she's going with this.

"Aiden didn't like me during the interview."

I cut her off and say, "He was a grade-A dick for no reason." I still remember how shocked I was at his unprofessionalism.

"I hit his car a week before," she blurts out.

"What?"

She can't stop grinning. "I was so embarrassed. It was a rough day. Like really bad and he backed up out of nowhere in the parking lot and I just tapped him." Her thumb and her pointer are parallel as she holds them up and whispers, "Just a teeny tap."

"You hit his car?"

"And then I might have… you know," she stops and laughs again. "I called him a dickhead when he was yelling at me. Like he was screaming in my face and it wasn't like it was helping anything and like I said, it was a rough day and I just snapped." Her shoulders shake with another giggle. "And then I showed up for the interview the next week."

"Oh my God! And you never told me?" I can't help laughing either. I can absolutely see Aiden and her screaming at each other in a parking lot over a scratch on a car. They both have a habit of taking out their aggression on the least suspecting.

"I was so embarrassed I couldn't tell you."

"Well no wonder he didn't want to hire you," I comment.

"I know. I had to go back in and apologize. I'd already sent him insurance information that he didn't even need, but still. I felt awful. It was so awkward and… unfortunate."

"But he still hired you," I say and hold up my finger to make that point clear.

"Because of you. He never would have if you weren't there backing me up."

"Knowing about the car... I'm going to have to agree with you now. I just thought he was an uncalled for asshole at your interview."

"I never told you and I want to thank you again, Beth. Thank you."

"Of course, I love you." I almost add how she was by my side through everything with Jenny before she died, and that getting her a job is insignificant in comparison, but I leave that out. I'm not wanting to drag the mood down.

"I love you too."

She spears her hand through her golden locks, moving all her hair to her left shoulder and glancing at her split ends. "You're off, like even more than you have been. And don't tell me *you're fine*," she says, mocking the words I've been giving her all night.

Reaching out for the bottle of wine, she gives me a pointed look. The swish of the liquid is followed by the sound of a car riding down the half-empty lot and I look at it instead of her.

Again not answering her. It's only about the dozen time she's asked me what's going on.

"A cop came to your house today." Her voice is clearer and when I look back, this time she isn't looking at me. I wouldn't call her expression a frown, it's something else, something etched with worry.

"When I was waiting for you to get home, which—by the way, where the fuck were you?" She pauses and sucks in a breath before relaxing into the seat and then taking another swig. She offers it back to me and then repeats, "I was waiting and a cop came by. I told him you weren't home and he said he'd come back later."

"Officer Walsh?" I question her and she nods, then takes the wine back before I can take another sip.

"I was going to tell you at dinner, but you seem really not with it. So like... I don't know."

This time I grab the bottle and take a drink before it's all gone.

Laura looks at me with a slight pout, although I'm not sure it's quite that. It's genuine and sullen, but there's a sadness I can't place.

I watch her look out to the shoe store we just left before she exhales with frustration. "You always tell me everything," she starts. "I know this is hard and you're not a 'speak your feelings' type of girl, which is ironic since you tell everyone else to do just that."

The wine flows easily until the bottle is empty, but I don't let it go.

"It just seems like this isn't mourning, it's something else and I don't know what to do or how to help you."

Laura's voice cracks as she raises her hands into the air, trying to prove a point but needing to wipe under her eyes instead.

"No, no, don't cry." My reaction is instant, reaching out to clutch her shoulder. The leather of her seats groans as I sit up and reposition myself on my knees to face her in the small car. "Everything's fine," I tell her but she only shakes her head.

With her eyes wide open and staring at the ceiling of the car, she responds, "It's not though. You're not okay."

"Seriously," I start to tell her and then catch sight of a car I recognize, and a prick I know too. Seth raises his hands in surrender at the wheel of his car, although his wrists stay planted on it, and my throat tightens. I can't hold on to my train of thought and I have to sit back in my seat, taking a steadying breath.

Jase sent Seth to follow me.

Maybe I should have guessed it. Maybe I should have known I'd be followed.

It's a strange thing, to feel safe, to feel wanted and protected by someone I know I fear and hate on a level that's unattainable to my conscious.

I rest my head against the cold window and close my eyes.

"We were having a good time," I tell her softly. Feeling the tingle of the bell, and falling back into old habits with Laura, I felt like I escaped for a moment. I'm nothing but foolish.

"Shit, no, don't you cry too." Laura presses a hand to her forehead and then over her eyes.

"I swear, I'm fine," I tell her although I can't help but to look past her and at Seth instead. "I…" I trail off and have to swallow before I lie again, "It's just hard to stop thinking about Jenny."

Fuck, that hurts to say. To use her as an excuse. To bring her up in conversation at all.

"And now we're both crying," I tell her with a huff and pull my sweater to the corner of my eyes. "I don't want to cry. It's just my eyes glossing over. It's not crying… I'm not crying."

"You're an awful liar." Laura's voice is soft and I'm pulled to her, to tell her everything. To lean on her like a friend would do.

How selfish is that?

"Tell me about work. I miss it. What kind of person misses work?"

Laura works in Human Resources at the center, but they get all the gossip just the same as the nurses who do the rounds like me.

"Well there's a cute guy who came in last week," she starts to tell me with feigned interest. Then her head falls to the side to look at me as she says, "But his name is Adam and we both know Adams are dicks."

Her comment forces a small laugh from me and then she reaches for the bottle.

"I don't know what's funnier, your taste in men or your pout when the wine's gone."

Instead of commenting, she pushes her hair back and tells me about a few new patients, all of which piss her off for good reason. A man who was drunk at the wheel and killed two people. She thinks he's faking insanity because ever since he was admitted all he can talk about is how totaled his truck is and he hasn't shown a damn bit of remorse for the couple he killed even though he knows he's being charged with their murder. We get those kinds of people sometimes. Assholes who fake mental illnesses to get out of legal trouble. Or even to get out of work for a week.

"Oh, I do love this one old woman who came in though. She said it's actually the 1800s and she's talking to dead people. I like Sue a lot. She's so sweet."

"I wish I were at work."

"I wish you were too," she adds and pats my thigh. "You'd love Sue."

"I'm sure I would." It's never a boring day at the Rockford Center. That's a truth no one can deny.

"I can't drive us home." Laura's statement makes me look at her and then at Seth. "You want to Uber?" she asks me and I shake my head no, getting out without thinking.

"What are you doing?" she calls out as I step out onto the asphalt and make my way to Seth's car. I ignore her calls for me to *get my ass back there*. I'd smile at the way she whispers it and tries to keep me from knocking on Seth's window if it weren't for the anxiousness creeping up on me from what I'm about to do.

I don't have to knock though; he rolls down his window but doesn't say a word.

"Oh my God, I'm so sorry," Laura says and tries to pull me away again. "My friend is a little bit more drunk than I thought." She tugs at my wrist and again I ignore her efforts.

"Will you give us a ride home?" I push out the question. Seth lets out a smile, a handsome smile with perfect teeth, all the while staring at Laura and her wide eyes.

"We don't need a ride," Laura's quick to tell him. "I'm so sor-"

"I don't mind," Seth cuts her off and asks, "Where are you going?" I'm still staring at Laura and the way she's looking at Seth that I don't notice he asked me.

"Home," is all I answer him and he nods once, the playfulness gone from his expression and tells us to get in the back.

I don't know what came over me or why. Maybe it's the piece of me that wants Seth to pay for watching me like a hawk. I can't explain it, but it feels like a step

A SINGLE KISS

forward. Not the literal step forward I take to get in the back of the car, but a step out of whatever place I was in just hours ago.

Laura snatches me when I open the door, and she immediately slams it shut instead. The thud is loud and nearly violent.

"What the fuck?" she hisses. "Do you even know him? Do you want to get us killed?"

"Yeah, I've met him a couple of times," I tell her and shrug, feeling like the worst liar in the world. A heavy weight presses against my chest as I escape the harsh wind, opening the door again and scooting over to the other side so Laura will get in too.

She takes a little too long to decide so I tell her, "Hurry up, it's cold out there and you're letting all that cold in here!" My admonishment works.

"Let me get my bag."

As she turns to walk away, Seth asks me all the while watching her, "Whose home?"

Whatever's settled into my stomach feels thicker. "Can you drop her off first?"

"You think she'd be okay with that?" He finally turns in his seat to look at me. "Because I don't."

I watch her texting on her phone a few spaces over with her driver's door open although she still stands on the street.

"I want to tell her," I admit to him. "You can stop me if I say something I shouldn't."

"You shouldn't say anything, Bethany."

"Well, I'm going to say something. I have to tell her." We both hear her car door shut and he says lowly, "You really shouldn't." The way his shoulders tense and he grips the wheel makes my chest feel hollow and I almost reconsider, but I have to tell her something.

She's my best friend and she deserves to know. I can't not tell her. I can't let her cry for me like she's doing.

Her car beeps from the alarm and then she's seated beside me, thanking Seth and referring to him as the "handsome savior" of our night although I can still hear the hesitation and worry in her tone.

She gives Seth a tight smile and then he asks again, "Where are you guys headed?"

"Can you take me to Jase's?" I dare to ask Seth, knowing Laura's going to ask me about Jase, paving the way for it to happen.

Seth's returning smile is tight, but he nods.

"Who's Jase?"

Ignoring Laura's question and her stare of confusion, I ask Seth, "Can you take Laura home first?"

"No fucking way are you staying in this car, drunk and with a guy you don't know." She glances at Seth who puts the car in reverse to leave as she adds, "No offense."

"He works for Jase," I answer her, finally looking her in the eyes.

"Who the hell is Jase?"

"Jase Cross," I tell her, gauging her expression when I mention "Cross." Everyone knows about the brothers and I can see the exact moment when it sinks in.

"You're with Jase?" she questions me softly and then swallows so loud, looking between me and Seth, that I'm sure even he can hear it. I only nod.

"With him? Like what does that even mean?"

My hands turn clammy and I have to wring my fingers around one another in my lap. "I can't even look you in the eyes," I tell her and then cover my face with my hands as my head sinks back into the seat.

"No, Bethy, no. Don't cry."

"I'm not going to cry," I protest, forcing my hands down and staring straight ahead at the back of the black leather seat in front of me. "I'm just..." I can't finish. "I don't even know what I feel. Ashamed, I think."

"Ashamed because you're with him? Or ashamed at what you've done?" she asks cautiously. She whispers, "Did he make you do anything? I will fuck him up. I don't care who he is."

"No, stop. No, he didn't make me do anything." Although I tell her that, the first time we met flashes in my memory. I think I'll leave that out of this conversation.

I have to shake out my hands, feeling them turn numb and having a wave of anxiousness hit me. "I'm ashamed because of both... neither. I don't know. I'm confused."

"Okay." Laura's patient with me although she keeps looking at Seth like he's not to be trusted.

The way she looks at Seth, questioning him and his intentions gives me an uncomfortable feeling. More than that, I feel like I should be defending them. Which is outrageous, yet it's exactly how I feel in this moment.

"He's a good guy," I tell her to ease her worries. "Jase treats me really, really good." Emotions tickle up my throat and I have to swallow them before I tell her, "Seth watches out for me for him."

She asks the obvious question. "Watches out for what?"

With Seth as my witness, I tell her everything.

I don't even leave out the part where I almost shot Jase. I tell her literally everything that I can remember. Including the part where I think I love him. Fuck my life.

CHAPTER 13

Jase

IT'S NOT EVERY DAY THAT I FEEL LIKE A PRICK.
Taking advantage of someone's weakness is how I survived, how my brothers and I rose to the top.

There's not a single doubt that I'm taking advantage of Bethany. It's easy when you're hurting to fall for someone, to trust them, to want there to be a way out of the pain.

Listening in on her conversation in the car, listening to her recount the events with Laura Devin, makes me feel like the worst fucking prick alive.

I made her love me. I made sure she had no other option. And worse than that, I don't know that I will ever say the words back to her.

"Boss." Seth nods when I see him and I nod back although my gaze travels to Bethany. Watching her climb the steps as I open the door for her.

Her cheeks are tearstained but there's a sense of lightness around her. Even more than that, her small body brushes against my chest as she walks in. She did it on purpose. She wanted to touch me and I fucking love it. Prick or not.

"Have a good night," I tell him and he smirks at me as he replies, "You too."

Bethany rocks from one foot to the other, watching me as I close to the door to the cold and then turn to her fully.

"Let me help you," I tell her and then act like a gentleman, helping her out of her coat.

With my fingertips lingering on her bare skin, I lower my lips to the shell of her ear and whisper, "Seth put you on speaker from the moment you knocked on his window."

She shudders from my touch and lets her head fall back into my chest. "Are you angry?" she asks with her eyes still open, staring past me at the now closed door.

"No, I'm not."

"I had to tell her." Her words slur slightly and I can smell the hint of alcohol on her.

"Of course you did."

"And you heard everything?" she asks and that's when her expression falls. No doubt she's questioning where my opinions lie. When I nod in response, she doesn't voice her question.

She takes a different approach, changing the subject altogether.

"What were you talking to Seth about before I went to him?" she asks me, her own curiosity showing.

"Maybe about you?" I give her a flirtatious response that's only a half lie, rather than telling her about Marcus.

"Oh... and what about me?" she asks although the flirtation isn't quite there.

"I wouldn't tell you, you like to gossip too much," I tease her, giving her a kiss on the crook of her neck. She rewards me by wrapping her arms around my shoulders, and planting one of her own on my neck.

The knowledge of what I'm going to do tonight keeps me from pushing for more. It keeps me from wanting more, it keeps me from lifting her ass up and pinning her against the wall.

"Are you okay?" I ask her, holding her close and not letting her go just yet.

"Me?" she questions and I nod against her, feeling her hair tickling along my stubble as I reply, "Yes, you."

"I feel better in a way," she confides in me and stands upright so I let her go. "It feels good to say it all out loud and still be able to stand afterward."

Staring into her gaze I admit to her, "You don't strike me as a girl who would ever not land on her feet, cailín tine."

"You know, I forgot to tell Laura that," she murmurs and sways slightly. Enough that she feels the need to take a step back and steady herself.

"How much did you drink?"

She shrugs and then says, "The normal amount when we go drunk shopping."

"No bags though?"

"Oh, well there's this thing where I owe this guy some money so I'm on a tight budget at the moment," she jokes with me and her smile is infectious. "Really, I just wasn't interested tonight in shopping."

"Only gossiping?"

"Yeah," she answers and then says again, "I can't believe I forgot to tell her."

Walking her to the bedroom, I ask her what she forgot to tell Laura.

"The nickname." Her answer stops me just outside the door although she continues, "I think she'd understand better, if she knew."

CHAPTER 14

Bethany

I<small>T'S DIFFERENT HERE. MAYBE BECAUSE IT'S HIS</small> room. His house. His place.

He's different here. He's more transparent. Less hidden with his emotions. Other than anger and dominance... and lust, he hasn't shown me more than that beyond these walls.

Or maybe it's just tonight. Maybe it's just the wine talking or the relief that I finally told Laura what's going on.

I don't know, but when I look at Jase, he's different.

And he's not okay. Pain riddles every move he makes. Not the physical kind, the kind that wears away at your mind.

His head hangs lower as he asks me what we did. As if he doesn't already know. His voice is duller, his grip less tight on my waist as he pulls me into the bedroom.

With every step my heart beats slower, wanting to take the agony away from his. The answers I give him are spoken without thinking. I'm more concerned with watching him than I am with making small talk.

With his back to me, he pulls the covers back and tells me to strip and get into bed, which I do.

My mind starts toying with me. Insecurity whispers in my ear, "*Maybe it's you.*"

"Are you okay?" I ask him, letting a tinge of my insecurity show.

"Fine," he answers shortly, but he gets into bed with me.

"You're still dressed," I comment, listening to my heart which is quiet. I think it's waiting for him to say something too. For him to tell us what's wrong.

"I know," is all he gives me as an answer and the high I was on, all that relief I felt, vanishes.

I feel sick. Not hungover or drank too much sick, but the sickness that comes when you know something's wrong. The awful kind where you can guess what it is, but you don't want to just in case it'll go away if you never voice it.

I know what I need, but I don't ask him for it. Instead I pull the covers up close around my chin and lie there. My pride is a horrid thing.

I'm aware of that.

If I could simply let it go, I could communicate better. I know that. I've known it all my life. But still, I don't ask him to hold me.

I don't have to though. I don't have to tell him what I

need to feel better.

The bed groans as he moves closer to me, wrapping a strong arm around my waist and pulling me closer to him. It's a natural reaction for me to close my eyes and let out an easy breath when I take in his masculine scent. It engulfs me just as his warmth does, just as his touch does.

"You promise we're okay?" I ask him and then my eyes open wide, realizing the mistake I made. The Freudian slip.

Kissing the crook of my neck, he murmurs a yes.

He gives so much and I feel so undeserving. The ringing on my skin comes back, the bell of what happened earlier reminding me that it's okay. That it's better than okay.

My hand lays over his and he twines his fingers with mine before planting a kiss on my cheek.

Before he can pull away, I kiss him again. Putting everything I have into it, trying to give him what I can in what's a very unbalanced relationship.

That's what this is. A relationship. Fuck me, when did it happen?

The second I pause, pressing my forehead to his and pulling my lips away, he does what I just did to him, kissing me and giving me more.

With a warmth flowing through my chest, I settle into his embrace.

"I want to ask you something." His whispered question tickles my neck and makes a trail of goosebumps travel down my shoulder.

"Yeah?"

"How are you feeling about your sister? Are you okay? You didn't mention her to Laura. Or how you were handling it. And the last few days you seem…"

"Seem what?"

"A little more than sad today before you went out and yesterday," he answers honestly, and I want to pull my hand from his, but he doesn't let me. He holds me tighter and closer as my composure cracks.

"Tell me, cailín tine," he whispers at the back of my neck, running the tip of his nose along my skin. I love it when he does that. I love the soft, slow touches. I love how he takes his time with me.

It takes me a long moment to answer him. "I feel like I've slowed down, which makes sense because I'm not working anymore. I am crying when I hate it and I can't stop myself, but that damn book is sad too, so it could be the book's fault right? I don't know."

"You can't hide behind a sad book," is all he says and then he looks at me like he wants more.

Staring at the still curtains and listening to the heater turn on with a click, I let it all out; I don't think, I just speak. "Everything is moving so fast. That's what it feels like. Like the world didn't just refuse to slow down with me while I mourn but it sped up too."

Kind eyes look down on me when I peek over my shoulder to see his response. He's propped up on his elbow, his hard, warm chest still pressed against my back. I roll over to face him and look him in the eyes as I say, "It became chaotic and unpredictable and I'm a person who likes consistency and schedules and predictability and it's all gone. In one second everything changed, and now I can't be anything but slow and everything is going so fast." He's silent, so I continue.

"Except when I'm with you. Everything slows down

then. It stops and waits for me when you show up."

I don't expect to say the words I've been thinking out loud. I say them all to my folded hands in my lap rather than to Jase. I need to see what he thinks though. If he understands or if I'm just crazy.

He leans down to give me a small kiss. It's quick and gentle. I want more but I don't take it. Even when the tip of his nose nudges mine, I don't do anything but wait for him to say something.

"That's a good thing, right?"

"Yeah... but I think the world is going so fast because of you too. Because of lots of things. And here I am stuck with a rope around my feet."

"I could see that," he comments, brushing the stray hairs away from my face and his touch brings back that tingling full force.

"You make it easy to talk," I murmur.

He doesn't say anything at all, he merely touches his fingers to my lips and gives me a small smile.

"I do that with my patients. I put on a smile all day long and they trust me, they open up to me. Jase, don't treat me like a patient."

"Well, first off all, you're not a patient. Second, you better not touch your patients like I touch you."

"You're awful," I tell him halfheartedly, but still feeling a hollowness in my chest that I can't place.

"I smile at you because sometimes you smile back, and that's all I want. I want to see you smile."

Breathe in, I remind myself. *Breathe out*. I have to, or else I think I'd forget in this moment. It's not often you can feel yourself falling, but I'd be damned if I didn't feel like that right now. Even knowing who he is and what he does.

"Why are you so sweet and charming… yet the very opposite too?"

He shakes his head gently, not taking it like I thought he would. Then he answers with another question of his own. "Why are you so strong and confident, yet… feeling like this?"

I don't have an answer. The old me would though. The me from only two months ago before Jenny went missing, would know why. I work in a psych center, for fuck's sake. I would have known. I could have answered. Being in it though… I've lost my voice. I have nothing to say, because I don't want this reality to be justified.

"Because that's life, cailín tine. We aren't just one thing. Life isn't one story. It's a mix of many and they cross paths sometimes."

I swallow thickly, understanding what he's saying and hating it. Some parts of life are simply awful. When I close my eyes and focus on one more deep breath, Jase's strong hand cups my chin and my eyes lift to his.

I nearly apologize for being the way I am. But it's not some stranger I've lost it in front of. Or my boss. Or my fucking family from New York. It's Jase.

I expect him to say something, but he only pulls me closer to him, letting time pass and the wretched feelings that have welled up, slowly go away.

Mourning is like the tide of the ocean. It comes and it goes. It's gentle and it's harsh.

Slowly, the tide always subsides. But it always comes back too. It never goes away for long.

"The world stops when you see me, huh?" he questions

softly after a moment, teasing me and letting the sad bits wash away like they're meant to. I love the teasing tone he takes. I love this side of him. I love many sides of him.

"I didn't say that," I'm quick to protest.

"You practically did," he teases, although the smile on his handsome face tugs down slightly as his eyes search mine.

"I don't love you," I murmur the words, feeling the hot tension thicken between the two of us. He leans closer to me, nearly brushing his lips against mine. All the while, I keep my eyes open, waiting for what he has to say.

"I don't love you too," he says and I can practically feel the last bit of armor fall as I lean into his lips. His hand brushes my shoulder, my collarbone and then lower, barely touching me and feeling like fire as he caresses my skin.

The covers swish around us as I lean back, giving him more room and urging him closer. I've never wanted a man like I want him. I've never memorized the rough groan a man gives as he kisses me like Jase does, with reverence and hunger.

I let him take me as he wants. What he wants is exactly what I want.

Time doesn't pause for us though. It doesn't go by slowly either.

It's all over far too soon. Maybe because I never want this one moment to end.

"I have to go," he tells me after glancing at the clock on his nightstand. He makes no effort to move though, other than to run his thumb along my bottom lip.

"Okay," I whisper, not wanting to chance that he'll stop touching me. All I want is for him to keep touching me and for my world to stay still and in pace with me, not wanting to take the next step forward.

"Don't follow me, Bethany," he warns, his voice sterner, but the lust still there.

"Okay," I repeat and my eyes finally close as he leans down, pressing his lips against mine once again. He tries to move away before I'm ready for him to go, but I reach up, pulling him back to me with my hands on the back of his neck. I hold him there, deepening the kiss and listening to his groan of satisfaction as I do. Kissing this man changes everything. I can't think about anything other than wanting him with me. I'm highly aware of it and I know it's dangerous, but still… I want it.

It's wild and dangerous, and I love it just as much as I love the fire.

When he finally leaves me, I hold on to the warmth he left in the covers, and I bury my head in the pillow he slept on, rather than the one he gave me. I stare at the clock, watching the hands move slowly. Trying to keep it moving slowly with me.

I don't follow him. Not because of a debt or an agreement. But because he asked me not to. Because it means something to him.

I would have stayed like that longer than I'd care to admit, really I would have, but that's when my phone chimed with a message from Laura.

CHAPTER 15

Jase

I KNOW HE'S HERE BUT HE HASN'T SHOWN HIMSELF yet. I say aloud to no one, "When I was a kid, I hated the dark."

The playground is quiet tonight. With its broken swing that creaks as a gust of wind blows, and the full moon's faint blue light that shines down and covers every inch of the fallen snow, it's the perfect setting for Marcus. The kind of setting that's eerily familiar. The place where you don't go and you walk as quick as you can to get far away.

The backyard playground of the abandoned school is where no one goes unless they're up to no good. Like I am tonight.

"Most kids do," a voice answers from somewhere to my right, under the old, ten-foot rusty slide. I can just barely make out the brown broken bits through the veil of snow.

"I figured you'd be there. In the dark, just watching." I make my way to where he is, but stop short. I stay by the swing set, close enough to hear, but not bothering to look at him.

I'll play by his rules. He has what I want, Jenny Parks. We both know that I know.

I can hear the faint laugh carry in the night, but he makes no other comment and instead there's nothing but the bitter cold between us.

"What about now?" he asks me and I resist the urge to turn my head to face where he is. Instead I stare at the graffiti on the back of the brick building.

"What about now?" I question.

"Are you still afraid of the dark?"

His question makes me smirk. "I never said afraid… I said I hated it."

"You didn't have to say you were afraid, Jase. Every child is afraid of the dark."

A moment passes and I stalk forward to lean against the metal bar of the jungle gym.

"You wanted something?" I ask him, knowing that my back is to him and knowing he could sneak up on me if he wanted. I'll risk it.

"You wanted something," he answers me as if it's a correction. His voice a bit louder this time, followed by the sound of footsteps. "Don't turn around just yet."

"Understood," I respond quickly, knowing in my gut I'm walking away from this. He wants me to know something. And I want to know what it is.

I can hear him stop just a few feet behind me and I stay where I am although the need to turn rings in my blood. I've never crossed Marcus and from what I know, he's never crossed me. But he isn't on our side either, and that makes me question where his intentions lie.

"You're looking for information and I came with… a gift."

My pulse quickens as I hear more movement behind me. Gripping the bar tighter until my knuckles have turned white, I ignore every need to turn, making my muscles tense.

"A gift?" I press him for more information.

"Yes," is all he gives me.

"Is it Jenny Parks?" I dare to ask, giving up information, but in the hopes of cooperation.

"Jenny is fine."

A beat passes and the muscles in my arms coil, my grip too tight, the adrenaline in my blood racing to get somewhere, or to do something. To simply react.

It's a puzzle with Marcus, attempting to ask the right questions, because he has all the answers.

"What are you doing with her?"

"I'm helping her." His voice is faint this time, as if he's farther away now. The crunch of the snow beneath his feet makes me realize he's pacing. Maybe considering telling me something.

"You know I want answers… I want her sister to have a life with her. She wants her back." There's only the soft call of a midnight wind that whistles in the lack of his answer. "What do you want me to know?" I ask him, acknowledging to both of us that's all he'll tell me anyway.

"Did you have a nice conversation with Mr. Stevens?"

An exhale of frustration slips through my lips at the

change in subject. I answer him, "It went well."

"What did he tell you?" he asks.

"He said you were building an army," I say and raise my voice to make sure he can hear me. He does the same and takes steps to come closer, but still stops far enough behind me that I can't see his shadow yet against the pure white snow.

"Building one?" The tone of his voice lingers in the air, and his answer leaves a chill to run down my spine. "Did you think I did all of this on my own? There's always someone looking for salvation, for redemption, for something to believe in."

"You're their savior?"

"I'm no savior and the things they do... it's no redemption."

"So you're using them?" I ask him and rein in the simmering anger as Jenny's face from the pictures in Bethany's house flickers in front of me. Back when things were different.

"I'm giving them what they want," he answers.

"And then?" I ask him. "What are you going to do with Jenny when she's done doing your bidding and you have no use for her?"

Silence.

My head falls forward, heavy as I struggle with the need to force an answer from the man I used to fear. I focus on staying still. On not facing him so I can gather more information. I need an answer. I need to know where Jenny is. I have to know if she'll ever come home.

"Did you know wolves used to live here? Back in the day, so to speak."

My eyes open slowly and I stare straight ahead as my shoulders tighten. "You love your stories. Don't you?" My voice is menacing, not hiding my disappointment and outrage.

"Oh I could tell you a story, but the truth will hurt the most."

My teeth grind together, my patience wearing thinner and thinner as all the pictures I've seen of Jenny from when she was a girl hugging her sister, to only a few years ago when she was in school, play in my mind.

"They'd run in packs and terrorize the people." He paces again, I can hear him doing it and a part of me wants to turn around; I want to look him in the eyes and see the man who plays with fire like he has. The only reason I don't is because he has the upper hand. He has Jenny. He has the answers.

"They attacked people, but farms mostly, leaving the families little food for themselves..." He pauses and lets out a soft sound, nearly a chuckle although I'm not certain it's humorous; it sounds sickening.

"They ruled and there was not much to be done. Much like you and your brothers," he says and the S hisses in the air. "They don't run wild here anymore though, because hunters found a way. Well, there were two ways." I remain silent, biding my time, struggling to stay patient with him.

"The first, I'm not a fan of," he says and steps closer to me, but still I don't react. "They'd find the female mates and put them in cages for the males to see. When the males would inevitably come to find their mates, they'd try to release them, to no avail. And then they'd wait there for the men to come, with their tails tucked under them, begging in whimpers for their mates to be freed." Every hair stands on end as he tells his tale. All I can think about is Bethany. "I've been told you didn't even need a gun to kill them when they did this. When they came to get their mates, they were so willing to do anything and accept anything in order to free their mates, you could turn your gun around and beat them to death with the end of a rifle."

My skin pricks with the imagery that floods my mind. The fog of my breath in front of my face paints the picture of a wolf, bloodied and dead and next to it a caged mate, with bullet wounds ending her life.

"Are you implying something, Marcus?" I dare to ask him, feeling the anger rising. "If you're threatening-"

"Bethany is safe," he answers before I can finish and the simple confirmation is more relief than I thought imaginable, given my current position.

"The other way though... I... I find it more fitting," Marcus says, and continues his story. "The farmers would dip a knife into bloodied water. Wolves love the taste of blood. They knew that, so they'd tempt them. They'd dip it and freeze it over and over. Practically making a popsicle, made just for wolves."

The swing blows and creaks again as he tells me, "They'd leave the knife for the wolves, and the wild animals would lick and lick, enjoying their treat and numbing their own tongues with the ice. They'd continuing licking, even after they'd sliced their own tongues. After all, they love the taste of blood and they couldn't feel it."

"The wolves would bleed out?" I surmise.

"They would. They would lick the knives even after the ice was long melted, and bleed themselves to death."

"Now, if only I'd heard that at bedtime, maybe I would have had better dreams," I lay the flat joke out for him, downplaying the threatening tone he chooses, and keeping my voice casual.

"Humor is your preference, isn't it?"

I don't bother answering.

"What's the point to your story, Marcus?" I ask him bluntly.

"I brought you a gift," he answers. "I brought you a bloody knife."

My jaw clenches as I wait for more from him.

"Trust me, you're going to want this one, Jase. I think you've been waiting for it for a long, long time."

"What is my bloody knife?" I ask him, gritting my teeth and praying it's not the body of Jenny Parks. That's all I can think right now. *Please, don't let it be her.*

"Inside the trunk of the lone car across the street is your package. I sent you a video, you should watch. He's had a high dose of your sweets. I'd think it'll wear off by tomorrow... Good luck, Jase."

CHAPTER 16

Bethany

"This is completely and totally shady," I mutter under my breath and then look over my shoulder to make sure no one saw me walk into the alley behind the drugstore. It's nearly 3:00 a.m. so the store is closed, as is everything else around here. "Could you freak me out any more?"

Meet me behind Calla Pharmacy. I have something for you.

That's the text Laura sent. And the messages afterward were a series of me asking why the fuck we were meeting there and her not answering my question, but insisting that I come.

"You have no idea the shit I was imagining on the way down here," I scold her although it's only concern that binds to the statement. The buzz from earlier has worn off completely, as if the current situation isn't sobering enough.

"Sorry." Laura's hushed voice is barely heard as she grips my arm and pulls me farther down the alley to where she parked her car.

"We can do shady shit at my house," I say, biting out the words.

"What if it's bugged or something?"

All I can hear is the wind as her words sink in.

Concern is etched in her expression as she looks back at me and then nearly opens her trunk, but she stops too soon and places both of her palms on the slick metal.

The streetlight from nearby barely illuminates us.

"It's dark and cold and you're freaking me out," I finally speak and ignore the way it hurts just to breathe in air this cold. I lift my scarf up to cover my nose before shoving my hands in my pockets and asking, "What the hell are we doing here?"

Every second it seems scarier back here. It's a vacant small lot, no longer asphalt as the grass has grown through patches of it. It's all cracked and ruined. Even though it's abandoned, there are still ambient noises. The small sounds are what spike my unease.

Like the cat that jumped onto the dumpster and the cars that speed by every so often out front. I should have told Jase. I should have messaged him, but I didn't.

"Why did we have to come down here? And why couldn't I tell Jase?"

"We just had to, okay." Laura's fear is barely concealed by irritation. "And he doesn't need to know about this. I did something," she quickly adds before I can get in another word. Her soft blue eyes are wide with worry and she looks like she can barely breathe. Her gaze turns back to the trunk and chills run down my arms.

"There better not be a body in there," I tell her more to lighten the mood, but also out of the sheer fear that she fucking killed someone. At this point, I don't know what to predict next.

"Jesus," she hisses. "I didn't kill anyone." She searches behind me and then over her shoulders like someone might be watching. "I'm not one of the crazies in your nut hut."

There's a small voice in the back of my mind telling me that Seth is somewhere. Seth is watching and Jase will know everything she says and does right now. But only if Jase knew I left, only if Seth is watching me nonstop. The thought is comforting for a split second, and then I regret not telling Jase.

"You promise you didn't say anything?" she asks and I nod.

I remind myself, this is Laura, Laura the friend I met in college, the girl who I ran to when I got dumped and needed to consume my weight in ice cream and fall asleep in front of romcoms. *My* Laura. My best, and really, my only friend.

There isn't a damn thing she could do that would be problematic. With that thought lingering, I get to the bottom of it. "Why are we here?"

"Look... first..." It's a heavy sigh that leaves her when she stares at me. The look she's giving me is begging for forgiveness and acceptance.

"You're freaking me out," I admit and grip her hands in

mine. They're cold, just like the air, like my lungs, like everything back here on the cold winter night. "Just tell me; I won't be mad."

Laura's never done anything like this and I don't know what to expect. I always know what she's going to do and say. She's the voice of reason more times than not. But this... "I have no idea what you did, but it's okay. Whatever you have to tell me or show me, it's okay." I hope my words comfort her like they do me. Even if they are only words.

"You have to accept it," she tells me and her voice is sharp. The worry is gone in her cadence, replaced by strength.

"Accept what?" The question I ask goes unanswered. Instead a breeze blows, forcing Laura's blonde hair to blow in front of her face although she makes no move to stop it. Bits of soft snow fall between us and all she does is stare at me and then make me promise.

"Promise you'll take it. Promise you'll never mention it again." She inhales too quickly and finally moves, shifting on her feet to look behind me before adding, "Promise it leaves with you and you forget where you got it."

My stomach coils and I nearly back away from her, but she grips my hand instead. "What the fuck is it, Laura?"

"Promise," she demands.

"Whatever it is, I promise." The pit in my stomach grows heavier as the trunk creaks open, darkness flooding it and hiding what's inside at first glance.

It's only when she pulls it out and shoves it into my chest that I see it's a black duffle bag.

The trunk shuts and the thud of it closing is all I can hear as I hold the bag. It can't be more than fifteen pounds, but until the hood is shut I have to hold it with both hands and then rest it against the flat back of the car.

"Don't open it. Just take it."

I look Laura dead in the eyes as I answer her, "You've lost your fucking mind if you think I'm not looking at what's in here."

"Don't. In case someone's watching."

"What is it, Laura?" I ask her again, my voice even but somehow sounding eerie in the bitter air.

"Your way out of the debt," is all she tells me until I grip her wrist, forcing her to look at me instead of walking back to her driver's seat like she intended.

She glances at my hand on her wrist, and then back up to me before turning to face me toe to toe.

I don't expect the words she says next. The casualness of her statement, yet how matter of fact it is.

"If you want to be with him, this is the world you live in. There's a risk of people going after you. If you don't… I think you're still in that world, regardless. It has a way of not letting go."

A silent shrill scream rings in my ears from the need to run, the need to do something. It comes from anxiety, from the need to fight or flee. I choose fight. I was born to fight.

She finishes, "But at least this gets rid of the debt."

It takes a second and then another for me to comprehend what she's saying.

"The debt? I owe him-"

"Three hundred grand." She nods as she speaks. "And now you have it to pay off."

"No fucking way." I'm adamant as I shove the duffle

A SINGLE KISS

bag into her chest but she doesn't take it, she doesn't reach out for it and the bag falls to the icy cracked ground. "Where did you get it?" I hiss the question, with a wild fear brewing inside of me. "Take it back," I beg her before she even answers.

Her baby blue eyes search mine for a moment and I'm left with disbelief and confusion.

I tell her with a furious terror taking over, "You don't have that kind of money."

"I didn't and then I did," she answers simply.

Emotions well in my throat. "Take it back, Laura. However you got it, give it back."

"No," she says first and then adds, "I can't anyway."

"No, Laura, fuck! No." I have to cover my face as it heats. "Please tell me-"

"I'm more than fine," she cuts me off. "I wanted to do something for a long time. An offer I had and wasn't sure if I wanted to take or not."

It's only the ease of her confession that settles me slightly.

"You can always go back."

"No," she answers me, "I can't and I don't want to. I'm not taking the bag back either and I have to go, I have the night shift and you promised me. You promised you'd take the bag."

"What did you do?"

"I can't tell you," she murmurs. There's no fear or desperation when she speaks to me and my head spins with the denial that this is even happening.

"You can, you can tell me anything." I feel crazed as I reach out to her, stepping forward as she steps back and kicking the bag at my feet.

"I can't tell you," she says, stressing every word and pulling herself away from my grasp. "That bag is yours. And I have to go."

She leaves me there with the duffle bag at my feet, the snow clinging to my hair and the cold of the night settling in to wrap its arms around me, the same way I wrap my hand around the strap to the duffle bag.

CHAPTER 17

Jase
Years ago…

I KNEW SOMETHING WAS OFF BEFORE I EVEN opened the door. I spent the hour before coming here arguing with Carter about even bringing Angie here.

I didn't trust her at The Red Room though. Not with the shit I have going on and the people that come and go. I tried to help her before and she took off, coming back worse. And the last three nights she destroyed the place, searching for anything to numb the pain she was in. She was fucking skin and bones. Her cheeks were so hollow. Addiction will do a lot of things to a person. It turns their curious smirks into glowers of pain, their bright eyes into dull gazes to nowhere.

It wasn't just the addiction though. She couldn't be sober because then she remembered what she'd done.

Fuck, the memory of it makes me sick.

"She's not with me, but that doesn't mean I can't help her."

"You can't help everyone, Jase." Carter's hardened voice is clear in my mind. He looked me in the eyes and told me, "You can't help her. You can't and shouldn't. You shouldn't have brought her here."

"I don't want to help everyone." I bit back the answer, feeling the anger rise inside of me. It was the first disagreement we'd ever had. I had to do it, though. "I want to help her. Just one person."

"Why? She's not yours."

He didn't get it. For the first time, he showed his confusion. He didn't understand that I didn't want her, I just wanted her to be okay. Even if she was nearly a stranger, even if I'd never want her to walk through the doors of the bar again once she left.

I needed to feel like I could make it right. We all make mistakes, but it's okay if you can make it right. I just needed to make it right.

"You shouldn't have brought her here." That was the last thing he said to me as I made my way back to the guest bedroom, questioning everything I'd done. I'd like to think that was why I thought things were off when I got to the door. But it was something deeper than that.

With my hand on the doorknob, I remember how I told her to just sleep before I left. Get some fucking sleep to help her with the withdrawal. Her eyes were so sunken in and dark as she screamed at me. It could have been the cocaine or the heroin. She looked nothing like the woman I'd known before.

I had to empty the room out to keep her from throwing

things. She liked comic books, so I went out to get her some. It would only be weeks. Only weeks of helping her get back on her feet, then she was someone else's problem. Then she'd be able to think clearly and choose whatever she wanted to do next. But as it stood, the addiction made every choice and it was leading her to an early grave.

I remember the way my scar shined on my hand, the light brighter there than on the metal knob as I pushed the door open.

It was quiet, too quiet for her not to be sleeping in the empty bed.

The bathroom door was closed and I glanced at the clock. 3:04 a.m. Someone once told me the Devil gets a minute every day. 3:07 to come and do his darkest deeds. I stared at the clock, knowing the Devil's deeds were done all day long, whether he was here or not.

Every second I sat on the chair in the room, I thought about what to tell her. I didn't know her well enough to know what to say. All I could think of telling her was that it would be better tomorrow. That she just had to take it day by day. It takes weeks to get through the worst of it, sometimes longer.

She didn't listen the first time, or the second, but maybe she'd listen now. Maybe tomorrow. Back then, I had hope.

The next time I looked at my watch, nearly forty minutes had passed. It was then that I realized it was still too quiet. Far too quiet.

I knocked at the door, but she didn't respond. "Angie?" I called her name, and still nothing.

I knocked harder, feeling that gut instinct that something was wrong. I remember the way her name felt as I screamed it and hammered my fist against the door, all the while, it was far too quiet.

Testing the knob, it wasn't locked, so I pushed it open. I knew then though, the Devil had come and gone. And that I was too late.

She'd shut the shower curtain, but even through it I could see the slash of red on the tiled wall. I'll never forget that first sound I heard that night when I went to check on her. It was the sound of the shower curtain opening.

The blood was all over her hands and arms. The first thought I had, was that she must've regretted it and tried to stop the blood from the cut at her throat.

She tried to take it back.

I didn't cry for her in that moment, but I leaned back against the wall, taking in her red hair and how it matted to her bloodied skin. Her eyes were still open, so once I could move, I closed them for her, even though my hand shook.

I failed her. I did this to her. It was all I could think.

Falling to my knees next to the tub, I prayed for the first time since my mama died. I asked God to take over for me. To help her and forgive her and forgive her sins.

I didn't ask him to forgive mine though. I'd be more careful about mine, but I knew I'd keep doing it.

I couldn't take back the years of what we'd already done. I couldn't take any of it back.

Carter was right, I never should have brought her there.

"I remember the first time I met Angie. I thought she was a sweet girl although a little too loud when she was drunk. She was older than me, and didn't want a damn thing to do with me other than to score drugs for a party. Which was fine, because the feeling was mutual." I talk easily, like I'm only telling a story.

"Coke or pot for the weekend. Whatever the flavor of the week was, she wanted it. It was easy to sell it to her. With her long red hair and wild green eyes, she wasn't my type, but I couldn't deny she was kind and polite. She used to stand on her tiptoes to turn around after getting her stash, doing a little curtsy of thanks that would at least get a chuckle from me.

"You remember Angie, Seth?" I speak clear enough that both Seth and Hal can hear me. The basement room today feels hotter than ever. More suffocating than it's ever been before.

"Of course." Seth answers calmly as I roll up the sleeves to my shirt. I'm careful and meticulous, but even so, I know I'm on edge. I'm on the verge of losing it and I haven't even touched the surface yet. He adds, "One of our first regulars," when I don't respond.

I made the mistake of watching the video Marcus sent me the second I got out of the park. I brought Hal here and waited. I didn't sleep, I didn't go home. I just waited until Seth said Hal was alert enough to go through with this.

Like always, he's standing behind Mr. Hal, who's in the interrogation chair. Although there's no interrogation today.

There are no questions for him. No need for a shirt to smother his screams. I want to hear them. I want the memories of tonight to somehow mask the memories I have of Angie's last day.

"You remember her?" I question Hal, feeling that crease deepen in the center of my forehead as I pick up the hammer. It's an ordinary hammer.

The tool of choice is fitting. Angie's dad worked as a carpenter. When he died, she went off the rails, that's what she told me once when she was struggling with her sobriety. It was easier than dealing with reality and the party drugs she bought for weekends became necessary every day. And then a few times every day. And then harder drugs. Just so she didn't have to think about her dead father.

So it made sense to me to choose a hammer.

"I don't know who you're talking about," the man answers. Confidently, stubbornly, like somehow he's got the upper hand here. Maybe he thinks I actually have questions, but I don't. All I have for him is a story.

I watch the light shine off the flat iron head of the hammer as I walk closer to him. There are no cuts on his wrists from trying to escape, nothing that shows any fear. And that's fine by me. I don't want him scared, I want him in pain. In fucking agony the way Angie was.

In the same agony Bethany's stuck in. The thought strikes me hard, and I hate it. I want it to go away. More than anything, I want her pain to stop.

My arm whips in front of me, the metal crashing against the man's jaw and morphing his scream into a cry of agony in a single blow.

The left side of his jaw hangs a little lower and the man fights against his restraints as he screams from the impact.

Glancing at the splatter of blood across my dress shirt, a huff of a breath leaves me, trying to calm the rage, trying to calm the need to not stop.

But Bethany's pain never stops. It never fucking ends.

"Marcus showed me a video. Only one. You knew her," I say and shrug, like it's not a big deal. Like he wasn't forcing himself down her throat while she was high and crying on a dirty floor.

"You knew her better than me," I comment. Thinking back to who she was before it all went downhill and trying to get the loathsome video out of my mind. If I could bleach it away, I would.

"She came in a lot, but only to get what she needed," Seth speaks from behind the fucker. He's reading me, his eyes never leaving me as I pace in front of the chair, waiting for Hal to stop his bitching and moaning.

"I want him to hear this," I tell Seth, raising my voice just enough for him to know not to console me like he's trying to do. I don't need that shit. I don't need to be told I couldn't have helped her or I couldn't have stopped it. I could have. I know I could have if I wasn't so fucking high on power and young and stupid. It's more controlled now. But back then, there was no protocol, and we sold to anyone and as much as they wanted.

"She was young, I had the drugs, I couldn't tell her no at first. She was the first person I told no. The first one where I realized I ruined her life." I'm staring at this asshole, and he's not looking at me. He's whimpering, looking down at his bare feet that are planted on the steel grid beneath him. He's not paying attention, so I swing the hammer again. Down onto his right foot. Crack! And then the left. The clang of the metal and the crack of small bones ricochets in the room. The black and blue on his skin is instant.

He screams and cries, but all it does is make me angry. He didn't care that Angie cried. He didn't care about what he did to her. He can mourn for his own pain all he wants, but it's not enough.

I have to walk away, seeing Bethany's face and knowing she wouldn't approve of this. What alternative is there though? To let this world turn with no consequence?

It's the fact that we feel pain when others feel nothing. This man feels nothing. The regret is hard enough and the guilt too, but walking around in a world where it isn't acknowledged, where those feelings travel alone… it's a hell that hides in every corner.

Hal cusses at me, spitting at my feet and sneering an expression of hate. He can't hold it long though. I slowly draw the sharp edge of the hammer across his throat as I speak.

"It was my fault, Hal. My fault that she got hooked and when she did, I sent her away. We'd only just begun in this game. We were bound to make mistakes. And Angie Davis was one of them."

Fuck, the guilt comes back full force just saying her name.

"I told her no, only a few months after I met her. I gave her the sweets, I told her to get better and then she could come back. Instead, she found you."

If she hadn't come to me, if Angie had gone to Bethany instead… My fiery woman, she would have known what to do. "Angie wanted help, she really did." I equate her to Jenny in this moment. Wondering if it really would have been different. If she really wanted help and if Bethany could have fixed her. I wish I could go back.

I can smash this hammer into his head, but I can't take her pain away. There's not a damn thing I can do to take Bethany's pain away

I think the words Hal's trying to say are, "Please, don't," as he spits up blood. It only reminds me of the way Angie said it in the video I saw hours ago. *Please, don't.*

"It's fine to party and have a good time, but she was slipping. She wasn't herself. Addiction grabbed hold of her and wasn't letting go. Anyone and everyone could see it."

"Yeah, I remember," Seth comments, nodding his head even as looks at me like he has nothing but sympathy for me. Fuck that. I don't need sympathy. I don't deserve sympathy.

"I remember. She was clinging to you crying, begging you for more." Seth still hasn't accepted what I have. Every word he says sounds like an excuse. "You sent her away with a way to help her."

Fuck, I should have known better. I wasn't in it like Carter was. I'd only just started and I didn't realize the ripple effect and the tidal wave it was capable of creating.

"I was young and I was stupid. I gave her whatever she wanted and however much she said she needed. Even when I knew it was getting bad. It took a long time before I sent her away..."

"Jase," Seth's tone is warning, cautioning me in where my mind is going, but I cut him off.

"No." My response echoes in the room even though it's pushed through gritted teeth while I tap the hammer in my hand, blood and all, as I add, "I take that blame. It's my fault. All of it."

Lifting the hammer up, I point it at Hal. "But you," I start to speak. I can't get the rest out though. I can't voice where this story inevitably turns.

Instead I crash the hammer onto his knees. Bashing

them relentlessly. Then his thighs. His arms. Every bone I can break.

Screams and hot blood surround me. The man's cries get louder and louder. Does he cry in front of me at the memory? Or at the realization that there's no way he's getting out of this room alive?

It's what I've wanted for so long, some kind of justice for Angie, but I thought it would feel different. I thought it would feel better than this.

Instead the pain seeps into my blood, where it runs rampant in my body. The memories refuse to stop.

With a deep inhale I back away, letting the screams dull as I think about how sunken in her face was when she came to me after a month of being gone. I didn't know. I didn't take responsibility for what I'd done, and I let her walk out, thinking she'd be fine.

Because that was the story I wanted to hear.

"She told me things you had her do, but you didn't have a name then. How you took advantage of her. You had others come in while she was tied down on the table. She told me how she didn't even care when you tossed the heroin at her. That she remembers how badly she needed the hit. Even as you and the other men laughed at her and what you'd done."

Seth isn't expecting the next blow I give to the guy, straight across his jaw. He lets out a shout of surprise as the blood sprays from the gushing wound, down Seth's jeans and onto his shoes.

The once clean, bright white sneakers with a red streak are now doused in blood.

He takes a step back, getting out of my way and keeping

his hands up in the air. He's acting like I'm the one who's gone crazy. But how could I be sane if the very thought of what happened didn't turn me mad?

"Seth, she ever tell you the things she did when we sent her away?" I ask him. Feeling a pain rip my insides open.

He shakes his head. His dark eyes are shining with unwanted remorse.

"She said she did shit she was so ashamed of, she couldn't tell me. She said she didn't deserve to live."

I smash the hammer down onto Hal's shoulder. But he doesn't scream this time and that only makes me hit him harder. Still, he's silent. His head's fallen to one side and I don't care. Maybe his ghost will hear me.

"All the money and all the power in the world, and I couldn't save her," I scream at the man. "You know why?" I keep talking to him. To the dead man. Feeling my sanity slip. "Why I couldn't save her?" I ask him, knowing Seth's eyes are on me, hearing his attempts to calm me down but ignoring him.

"Because she couldn't live with the things she'd done when she wasn't sober. She remembered it all. And she couldn't deal with it."

There is never true justice in tragedy.

You have to live with yourself after what's done is done.

"Angie couldn't do it," I tell him. "She couldn't live with the memories and she couldn't forgive herself."

I locked her in a room to help her get over the withdrawal. I gave her the pills and I gave her a safe place.

She killed herself.

"She had a sister. She had a mother who needed her. I couldn't even get out of the car at the funeral because of how they were crying."

It's the endings that don't have an honest goodbye that hurt the most. They linger forever because the words were never spoken.

I don't know who I'm talking to at this point. Seth or a man who didn't feel remorse for what he'd done, only for himself. I should have made him suffer longer. I should have controlled myself.

I hate that I ever sold her anything. I hate that the beautiful redhead at the bar would never smile again. All because of a dime bag of powder that took her far away from the world she wanted to leave. All because I sold it to her.

Every blow, I would take too. I deserve it.

Bethany should do to me what I've just done to this man. I led Jenny down that path. We sold her drugs, we bribed her with them for information. Even if it wasn't her first or her last, I know we sold her something and then let her walk away.

The thought only makes me slam the iron of the hammer down harder and more recklessly. Crashing into his face, his shoulders and arms. Every part of him. Over and over again, feeling all the anger, the pain, the sadness run through me, urging me to do it again and again.

When my body gives out and I fall to the floor on my knees, heaving in air, I finally stop. Letting my head fall back, and closing my eyes.

I could never tell Bethany. She deserves to hate me. I don't deserve her love, let alone her forgiveness. Not any of it.

CHAPTER 18

Bethany

THE VERY IDEA OF LEAVING THREE HUNDRED thousand dollars in the back of a car makes me want to throw up. People kill for this kind of money.

I can hardly even believe I actually have that amount. I didn't count it and I don't intend to. I don't want to touch it. All I did was unzip the bag once and then close my eyes again, pretending like I didn't see it.

Three hundred thousand dollars. I don't know what Laura did to get this money, but maybe I can give it right back to her. I don't think Jase gives a shit about the debt. A very large part of me believes it's more than that.

I won't know until I do this. Although sickness churns inside of me at the possibilities, I focus on the one thing I want to happen. I hand it to him, telling him honestly where it came from. He hands it back, telling me it's not my money and he doesn't want it.

"That's what will happen," I say for the dozenth time under my breath to no one. Maybe the dozenth is the trick, because I'm starting to believe it.

He wasn't home when I got back last night and he wasn't home when I woke up after only sleeping a handful of hours. He didn't answer my texts. He's nowhere to be found. The money was in the car while I paced inside waiting and waiting. I finally had to come out and make sure it was still there. I ended up getting in, just to kill time rather than pacing and pacing. I drove past the graveyard a few times, but I never got out of the car.

Pulling out the keys from the ignition, I stare up at the large estate, going over the dialogue in my head one more time.

The debt is paid. The time we had together was time I spent with you and nothing more and nothing less. That's what I'm going to say to him. I can do it.

I'm burning up in the car, the sweat along my skin won't quit. I know part of it is from the duffle bag in the back. I look over my shoulder once again, just like I have the entire drive down here last night and even an hour ago to make sure it didn't magically disappear.

Part of this anxiousness though is because I don't know what Jase will say or what he'll do with me once the money's handed over.

It's not just a debt. I know that. It can't be just a debt to him.

Opening the car door lets the cool air hit me and I relish in it. Calming down and shaking out my hands.

This world Jenny brought me into... I'm not fighting it anymore. I'm walking into it, ready for what it will bring me. It's another step forward. I can feel it. Just like telling Laura everything. Maybe it's a small step, but it's one I'm taking.

My heels click on the paved path to his door. The door that I open on my own.

He could take that away, but why would he? The doubts swirl and mix with the fear that what we have is only about the debt. Maybe he likes holding it over my head; maybe he thinks he won't have the upper hand if I pay it off.

That thought actually eases the tension in me. He's never going to have the upper hand when it comes to me. He should know that by now.

Calm, confident and collected I walk into the foyer and then past the hall, listening to my heels click in the empty space. The clicks, the thumps, they all only add to the urgency to tell him. To get it off my chest and to get that cash out of the back of my car.

"Jase," I call out his name, seeing the bedroom door open, but he doesn't answer.

A chill follows me, bombarding me even as I stand in the threshold of the dark bedroom and see only the light from the bathroom.

There are moments in time when you know instinctively everything is wrong. You know you're going to see something that you don't want to see. It's like there's a piece of our soul that's been here before. A piece that's preparing you for what's to come. Warning you even. And maybe if I was smarter, I'd take the warning and I wouldn't step foot into his bedroom.

I'm not smart enough though.

With the sound of running water getting louder as I approach, I creep quietly to his master bath.

The water's so loud I'm sure he couldn't hear me. That's what I tell myself.

Thump, my heart doesn't want to be here. *Thump*, it wants me to stop. I test the doorknob, and it's not locked. Something inside of me screams not to take this step. Not to go forward. *It's the wrong time, I'm not ready for it.* I can feel it trying to pull me away.

But I'm already turning the knob and with a creak, I push the door open.

I catch sight of his clothes on the floor first; he's still hidden from view from where I'm standing. The mix of bright and dark red splotches and smears wraps a vise around my lungs.

I can't breathe, but I still move forward.

Blood. There's blood on his shirt. That's blood, isn't it? Fear wriggles its way deeper inside of me, like a parasite taking over.

"Jase," I barely speak his name while taking a small step forward. My gaze moves from the blood on his clothes piled on the tile floor, to his naked body seated on the edge of the tub. He's covered with the way he's sitting, and his head's lowered, hanging heavy in front of him. I'm not sure he heard me the way he's sitting there. Like he's stunned, like his mind is elsewhere, lost in another place or another time.

Despair is crippling and I swallow hard. My trembling fingers reach out to pick up his shirt, wanting to believe it's not blood. There's not a mark on his skin, no cuts or bruises that are fresh. The cut I gave him is scabbed over.

The warmth of the air flows around me as I step closer and lift the shirt off the floor. It can't be blood, Jase isn't injured. Jase is fine.

But it looks like it. I don't understand. There's so much blood, in different patterns. Smeared and stained into the undershirt. I still don't want to believe it. I wish it would be anything else. My head spins as I grip the shirt tighter, staring at it as if it'll change, it'll go back to being clean if only I look at it the right way. But it's blood. There's so much blood, my hands are wet with it.

"Bethany." Jase's voice catches me off guard and I scream, pulling the shirt into my chest out of instinct before shoving it away when I realize I've pressed the bloody clothes to my own.

I could throw up with the revolting disgust and fear that sink into my bones. The blood is on me.

"Whose blood is that?" The question tumbles from me as I take a step backward and Jase stands up tall. My hands grip the doorway and my fingers leave a trail of blood.

There's a look in his eyes I will never forget when my gaze finally reaches his.

A darkness I haven't seen before and the fear that accompanies it is all-consuming.

In sharp spikes, the chills take over and I take another step back. Out of the bathroom and away from him.

That piece of my soul that was warning me before… it wasn't about the blood, it was about Jase. I know it to be true when he takes another step forward, so much larger than mine with his hands raised and he tells me to calm down.

If I could speak, I'd tell him he's crazy to think I should

calm down. If I could speak, I'd scream at him, demanding he tell me what he's done.

But I can't. Every syllable catches in the back of my throat in a way that feels like I'm choking.

"Let me get a shower and we can talk," Jase states calmly, the savage look in his eyes just barely dimming.

My head shakes, all on its lonesome and I turn and run. As fast as I can, I run away from him.

"Fuck," I hear him mutter as I bolt to the door, sweeping myself around it and crashing into the hall wall. I don't stop running, even though I don't hear him behind me.

Thump, thump, thump, thump. My heart pounds faster than my heels, ushering me away.

As I reach the door, I hear him call out. With my hand on the scanner, I turn around to see him with a pair of sweats, walking toward me, not running.

Maybe he thought that would keep me from leaving. Maybe he thought I wouldn't be threatened or I wouldn't be scared.

But he was wrong.

So fucking wrong. The second I swing the door open, I hear him scream my name and start running. I slam the door closed knowing he'll have to use the scanner too. It's another second I have ahead of him. Only seconds.

Run!

I scramble to my car and to find my keys. With terror raging through me at Jase getting his hands on me and forcing me back inside, at not knowing what he'll do to me or what he's capable of, I shove the gear into drive and reverse out of the driveway. I'm senselessly speeding away with the sight of him swinging the door open the moment my car hits the gate. Crashing it open and denting the hood of my car.

Even as I scream, I keep my foot on the gas, not caring about the damage, just needing to leave as quickly as possible.

I need to run and never stop.

Run far away and not look back.

The car jostles as I go over a curb and then another, my tires screaming as I race out of the long drive and backroads to get to the busy streets.

My gaze spends too long in the rearview, waiting for his car to show. It doesn't, but that doesn't keep me from tearing down the road.

My grip is hot, my pulse fast. I need to get the fuck out of here.

It's only once I've gotten onto the main road and I'm minutes away from my home that I let myself think of anything other than the need to go faster.

How could I love him? How could I want to love him?

Thoughts run wild in my mind, fighting with each other to be heard. There's a pounding in my temple and I don't even realize when I've run the red light until a car beeps their horn at me.

Fuck! I have to veer to the right to miss hitting the SUV. A wave of heat flows over my skin, far too hot as my tires squeal and I barely keep my car on the road.

That doesn't stop me. I keep going. I don't stop. I can't stop. I need to go faster. I need to get away.

With my chest heaving, I catch sight of the blood. Oh my God, the blood.

I need to get it off. I need to get this off. Bile climbs up my throat and I have to swallow it as I pull into my driveway. It's a reckless turn but I don't care. I need to get inside and get this off.

Get this blood off of me. Get Jase Cross off of me.

It's all I can think about as I slam the door shut to my car and run to the porch. The gust of cold air brings with it the white mist of an incoming storm tonight.

My hands are still shaking as I search for my key and that's what I'm staring at when I hear Officer Walsh's voice. "Bethany?"

The surprise and shock make me scream and drop my keys. They bang as they hit the ground and I stay perfectly still.

"Fuck." The word is spoken faintly as I stare back at him on the other end of my porch as he gets up from the chair. Like he was waiting for me.

I know my expression is one of fear and guilt, a doe-eyed woman caught in the act of something awful and I can't change it as our gazes lock.

"Is that blood?" he asks, standing straighter, but with his hand behind him as my feet turn to stone and refuse to move.

"No," I lie and his head tilts as his hand pushes his coat back and his fingers rest on his gun.

"I didn't do anything," I spill the words out, pleading with him to understand. My pulse rages and I can barely stand up straight. Fuck, no. How did this happen?

"Tell me everything. I can help you," he urges, but it doesn't sound sincere.

"You have to believe me. It's not me. I didn't do anything."

"Tell me whose blood that is."

"I don't know," I practically shriek.

"It is blood then?" he questions. Immediately, I feel caught. I feel trapped. The bite of the air creeps in, cracking the heat that's consumed me.

My lips part, but instead of giving him words, all I can do is swallow as my vision becomes dizzy.

"Tell me everything, Bethany; what happened?" His question comes out harder this time and he takes a step forward. I instinctively take a step back and my back hits the wall of the house.

With a trembling voice I whisper, begging him to let me go. "I can't," I tell him. "I don't know."

My inhale is ragged as he takes another step closer and I have nowhere to go.

"I wish I didn't have to do this." Pulling out the cuffs from behind his back, he tells me, "Bethany Fawn, you're under arrest."

Jase and Bethany's book concludes in … *A Single Touch*.
Their final book.

There are many moving parts in this world. If you haven't read Carter's saga, starting with *Merciless*, I highly suggest you do that now. His story is just as intense and a tale that will stay with me forever. I hope these words stay with you as well.

Here's to love stories keeping our hearts beating.

ABOUT THE AUTHOR

Thank you so much for reading my romances. I'm just a stay at home mom and avid reader turned author and I couldn't be happier.

I hope you love my books as much as I do!

More by Willow Winters
www.willowwinterswrites.com/books

Printed in Great Britain
by Amazon